THE WIND RIVER KID

THE WIND RIVER KID

WILL COOK

THORNDIKE
CHIVERS

This Large Print edition is published by Thorndike Press, Waterville, Maine, USA and by BBC Audiobooks Ltd, Bath, England.

Thorndike Press is an imprint of The Gale Group

Thorndike is a trademark and used herein under license.

LIBRARY OF CONGRESS CATALOGING-IN-PUBLICATION DATA

Cook, Will.
    The wind river kid / by Will Cook.
      p. cm. — (Thorndike Press large print western)
      ISBN-13: 978-0-7862-9791-7 (lg. print : alk. paper)
      ISBN-10: 0-7862-9791-3 (lg. print : alk. paper)
      1. Large type books. I. Title.
    PS3553.O5547W56 2007
    813'.54—dc22   2007017968

BRITISH LIBRARY CATALOGUING-IN-PUBLICATION DATA AVAILABLE

Published in 2007 in the U.S. by arrangement with
Golden West Literary Agency.
Published in 2007 in the U.K. by arrangement with
Golden West Literary Agency.

U.K. Hardcover: 978 1 405 64256 9 (Chivers Large Print)
U.K. Softcover: 978 1 405 64257 6 (Camden Large Print)

Printed in the United States of America on permanent paper
10 9 8 7 6 5 4 3 2 1

THE WIND RIVER KID

1

She sat erect on the seat of the buckboard, handling the reins like a man, with her wrists stiff, her elbows tight against her sides. She wore a gray linsey dress and a bonnet tied firmly over copper-hued curls. The backs of her hands were deeply tanned, as was her oval face; a sprinkling of freckles peppered the bridge of her nose. She was young in years, but a lifetime in a rough land had driven the nonsense out of her until she carried a perpetually grave expression around her full mouth.

While she drove, she studied the land: sheer mountain rises, thickly furred with tall pine and Douglas fir, with the winding road the only visible scratch on the virgin face. The road wound beneath the buckboard's ironshod wheels, clinging at times to a bare foothold on the mountain's face.

Finally the road made a sharp turn and dipped quickly to a valley floor where the town of Rindo's Springs lay, close-huddled, the hub for a large planing mill, a saw camp, and the huge lumber company buildings. On the other side of the town, a slab burner rose to a high cone, belching an eternal cloud of smoke. Distance did not muffle completely the rip of power saws, the moaning roar of planers.

She drove patiently, letting the miles fall behind her as she left the four-mile downgrade and entered the town. Rindo's Springs was a cross-hatching of narrow streets flanked by heavy log buildings and uneven boardwalks. In the air were the tangy flavors of pitch and coal smoke from the huge steam engines at the company mill.

A recent rain had left the road thick and sticky, and the buckboard's wheels flung mud as she navigated the street. The peeled logs of the buildings were darkly damp, and as she passed the corner saloon, she came under the sharp scrutiny of the porch loungers. She held the team to a slow walk for the length of the street; not that she felt like taking her time, but because she was a woman sharply aware of public opinion and constantly on guard lest unseemly behavior color their judgment of her.

Besides, the streets of Rindo's Springs were too crowded for speed; nearly everyone within a radius of twenty miles was in town. Buggies and saddle horses were packed together, and there was not a single empty place along the main drag's hitching racks.

Aside from the sounds coming from the saw camp, the town was strangely silent; the men who stood along the boardwalk's length did not speak to each other; they presented only a solid-faced patience. She nodded to many, her own men, and ignored the others.

She turned at another side street and pulled up to the hitchrack in front of the jail. Dismounting, she tied her team, then crossed the walk and opened the door without knocking.

The sheriff raised his eyes quickly, then smiled as though relieved. He had a newspaper spread on his desk and his revolver lay disassembled, a scattered pile of oily, metal parts. The girl leaned her back against the heavy plank door. "Ben, with a town full of enemies this is a poor time to take your gun apart."

Ben Colfax leaned back in his chair, his fingers searching his vest pockets for a cigar. He was fifty-some and feeling his age. Tired lines were etched permanently on his face. Even the badge pinned to his shirt front looked tarnished and ready for retirement.

"I have no real enemies," he said mildly. "It's just that a man caught in the middle has no friends." He looked steadily at her, a genuine affection in his eyes. "The voting is over, Bess. Just a matter of waiting now while Judge Richmond and the mayor count the ballots."

"How do you think it's going to go?" she asked.

Ben Colfax sighed and brushed his revolver parts aside to make a place for his elbows. "I went over the voting register pretty close, Bess, and except for the merchants, it's a fifty-fifty chance." He shook his head sadly. "Was your father alive, I'd say we had Rindo licked. He had as much power among his faction as Rindo does in his. But now there's no telling which way the merchants will go. Rindo's direction, probably." He took his cigar from his mouth and brushed his shaggy mustache. "Wish I could help you, Bess. You know I wish that, but I can't."

She pulled a heavy chair close to Colfax' desk and sat down. "Ben, no one on this earth will ever make me believe that Cadmus Rindo didn't kill Pop, or have him killed. And just five days before the election — that's too convenient, Ben. Too close to be coincidence."

10

He reached across the desk and patted her hand. "Bess, I've been a lawman all my life. I respect the law, and the law heard all the evidence I could gather against Rindo, and the law said he was innocent." He spread his hands. "I've got to respect that judgment, Bess. And you have to respect it."

"I'm going to fight that old man," she said flatly. "Fight him as hard as Pop ever did."

"But keep it legal," Ben Colfax said gently.

She stepped to the door and paused there. "Ben, do you think Cadmus Rindo's keeping this election legal? Who is this man Onart? None of us have even seen him. Have you seen him?"

"No," Ben Colfax admitted. "I haven't. He's just a name on the ballot."

Some of her resentment and hurt vanished as she regarded this kindly man; her voice grew soft. "Ben, you just refuse to see bad in anyone, don't you?"

"Easier to see the good," he said. "I guess I'm weak."

"No," she said. "You're very strong, Ben. And I wish I had some of that strength right now." She stepped outside and closed the door. Turning east, she moved along the warped boardwalk, lifting her skirt and feet carefully so as not to stub a toe on the irregular cracks.

This was a lumber town and the men here were like the timber they hewed, tall and generally big-boned, silent men for the most part, but today the silence was unnatural. She nodded to a few of her friends, but did not stop to speak to anyone. Somehow, all talk seemed used up. The buzz and commotion from Rindo's company lot held the men's attention, for earlier in the day he had closed down for a half-hour so his employees could vote. Now it seemed that they were totally disinterested in the election's outcome, as though they already knew which way it would fall.

The polling place was Murray Burkhauser's log saloon and a group of men stood on the porch. Murray Burkhauser was there, his hands thrust into his pockets, a fine cigar fragrantly ignited between his teeth. He was a tall man, although not overly heavy. Timber had never been his business, and although he had lived in this town four years, he was as out of place as a total stranger, a man in alien surroundings. Kansas City or San Francisco would have been more to Murray Burkhauser's liking, a chandeliered palace with dancing girls and a dozen sweating bartenders, and customers in beavers and ascot ties. Not a log building festooned with elk antlers and smoky ceiling beams, with a banjo and a tinny piano. Yet, for reasons he discussed with no man, Murray Burkhauser had no intention of leaving Rindo's Springs.

When Bess stepped onto the porch, he said, "Too bad women can't vote, although I doubt one more could make a difference now."

She gave him a steady look, holding her temper back. Her glance shifted to the man standing on Burkhauser's left. "You're looking smug, Cal."

"I don't mean to be," he said. He was a young man in his early thirties. His eyes were a deep brown and his skin a tightly stretched covering for good bones. Unlike Murray Burkhauser, Cal Runyon *was* timber, but not the two-dollar-a-day, fall, limb, and buck kind. Timber boss was closer to it, for he wore a pair of cord trousers and engineer's boots, and a manner that automatically told an observant man that he was well paid to exercise authority.

"Where did you find this dark horse Onart?" Bess asked.

"I didn't. Cadmus Rindo picked him." He pulled out a stem winder and glanced at it. "The count should be finished pretty soon." He touched her lightly on the arm. "Will you step inside?"

Her impulse was to refuse, but everyone on the porch looked at her. Bess shrugged and stepped through the door. No liquor was being served, both Rindo and Ben Colfax having agreed beforehand to keep the election a sober one. Along one wall, planed pine booths had been installed, and Cal Runyon led Bess to one. She hesitated, then sat down. Cal Runyon slid in across from her.

"Bess," he said softly, "you're holding a hate as though you liked it."

"Pop's dead," she said dully. "He was all I had left, Cal."

He made a waving motion with his hands, as though searching his mind for a way to get through to her, to crush her prejudice. "You won't listen to me, will you?"

"Why should I?" she asked. "Cal, you work for Rindo, and he was the only man who stood against Pop."

"But not to the extent where he'd kill him," Runyon said. "The old man loves a fight, Bess. But an open fight. Not a shot in the dark."

She placed her hands flat on the table, preparing to rise. "I buried him the day before yesterday, Cal. It's too soon for me to listen to you."

"Would I lie to you?" he asked. "Bess, do

I have to tell you how I feel?"

"No, and I don't want to hear it." She stood up and looked at him. "Cal, I'm afraid to trust you now. Almost afraid to trust anyone." Quickly she turned and walked to the door. But there a thought halted her and she came back. "Can I ask you something straight out and get a straight answer?"

"I've always answered you straight," he said.

"Then who is Onart and why hasn't anyone seen him?"

Cal Runyon studied his hands for a minute. "Bess, the old man was mad, at you and at Ben." He looked steadily at her and there was an appeal in his eyes. "I tried to talk him out of this, but he went ahead anyway, putting this man against Ben."

"Ahead with what? Cal, you're not answering me. Where is Onart? No one's seen him."

"He's in jail," he said softly. "Bess, I'm sorry."

Her eyes went wide with disbelief. "Cal, this is a joke!"

He shook his head. "No joke, Bess. I wish it was."

Anger began to fan a warming heat into her face. "Where's Cadmus Rindo now?"

"You'll find him at the hotel," he said. She

whirled and hurried out and Runyon got up to go to the door as though he meant to follow her.

Bess turned north along the boardwalk, and at the next corner she crossed over. The two-story hotel sat on the corner, the wide lower gallery fronting the boardwalk. Cadmus Rindo sat in his favorite chair. He was a man nearly eighty, but age had not undermined his spirit nor dulled the razor edge of his mind. His hair was white as was his beard, but he looked at Bess Jamison with the drill-sharp eyes of a much younger man.

"What kind of a man are you?" Bess asked.

"Whatever people make me be," he said flatly. "So you found out about Onart, huh?"

"That was low," she snapped, "running a jailbird against a man like Ben Colfax."

Cadmus Rindo laughed without humor. "Does make Ben look pretty bad, don't it?" Then his laughter vanished. "But keep in mind that Onart ain't a jailbird. Just a common drunk."

She regarded Cadmus Rindo with eyes that mirrored her disbelief. "Why don't I just get a gun and shoot you?"

"Was you a man," Rindo said calmly, "I'd have given you your chance at the inquest the other day." He leaned forward and speared her with his eyes. "A woman ought

to stay at home. Get married. Have babies."
His eyes pulled into narrow slits. "Stop
meddlin' in a man's business." A smile
began to lurk behind the snowy thicket of
whiskers. "I'll miss your pa. Always gave me
a fight for my money."

"You'll find that I can put up a scrap too,"
she said softly. "And you've given me added
reason, old man. What you've done to Ben
Colfax will break his heart. What kind of a
man are you to do such a thing?"

"Like any other man," he said. "Any damn
fool can win a friend, and lose him the same
day. But when you break a man's spirit, you
achieve something absolute."

"I guess that's your crowning achieve-
ment, isn't it? You own the town, the biggest mill, the freight line, and the logging
railroad. Now you own the law, all bought
and paid for. I suppose you'll make that
gunman, Pete Davis, a deputy."

His eyes grew dark and there was an angry
set to his cheeks. "Now you understand
something. I didn't want to own the sheriff,
but you and Ben Colfax made me buy him
for my own protection."

"You're completely rotten," Bess said and
mounted the porch. She went directly to
the clerk's desk, took a key to a room on
the second floor, and walked up the steps.

Rindo's last remark still stung her and beneath her breath she called the old man many names, and branded him a coward for seeking someone else upon whom he could place the responsibility for his acts.

She could understand why Onart's identity had been kept a closely guarded secret; Rindo's men would vote the way he told them to vote, and Bess's employees would vote for Ben Colfax, regardless of who was running against him. Rindo, she knew, must have guessed that once Ben found out who his opponent was, he would simply have resigned, thereby depriving old man Rindo of his moral victory.

Locking the door, she stripped off her dress and washed her hands and face. Then she sat down on the bed to think, trying to figure out the most gentle way to tell Ben Colfax about Onart. Yet there didn't seem to be a way. She left the bed.

Through the open window she could hear the sounds of laughter along the street; the quit whistle blew at the mill. While she stood there, watching, every man on Cadmus Rindo's payroll drifted into town, clogging the main street, filling the town with swagger and loud talk. She could see her own men down there, easing aside for Rindo's men. Had the election swung toward

Colfax, her own men would be kings of the street, filled with victory-built confidence. But defeat robs a man of his strength and makes him unsure of himself; she could not blame her men for drifting to the end of town.

The citizens of Rindo's Springs were staying clear of the traffic. Their vote had been swayed by Cadmus Rindo, and now that the election had teetered his way, they were content to make the best of it. Burkhauser had opened the saloon for business and the bulk of the crowd gathered there.

She saw Cal Runyon leave the saloon porch and walk diagonally across the street toward the hotel. He looked up toward the upper gallery and spoke briefly to Will Beau-Haven, who owned the place, then passed from Bess Jamison's sight beneath the overhang.

She slipped into her dress quickly as knuckles tapped against her door. She crossed the room, one hand fastening buttons; the other turned the key. Cal Runyon stood there, hat in hand. "You going to let me come in, Bess?"

She nodded and stepped aside. He waited while she closed the door, then tossed his hat on the chest of drawers. He smelled strongly of shaving soap and pipe tobacco

19

and the timber. His face was a canvas on which worry was clearly painted. "Ben knows by now. Some of the boys went to the jail to rub it in." He lifted his hands in a feeble gesture. "I couldn't stop them."

"Did you even try?" She glanced at him briefly, then turned away. "What's the use of even talking about it, Cal?"

"We don't have to be at each other's throats, do we?"

She turned to him suddenly. "What do you want of me, Cal?"

"To marry me," he said simply. "Let Cadmus have the damn place."

"Did he send you here to ask?" Her anger was like an explosion, quick to spring up and quick to die. His expression tightened and she was instantly sorry. "Forgive me, Cal. I didn't mean that."

"It's all right," he said.

Shaking her head, she reached up and brushed the bronze curls away from her forehead. "It's not all right. We're starting to accuse each other. Before we know it, something will be said that we can't forgive. I don't want that to happen." She turned and looked again out the window. "It's not pleasant, knowing that you're beaten. Have you ever known the feeling?"

"No," he admitted. "Things have been

easy for me."

She looked around quickly. "Tell me the truth — how can you work for a man like Cadmus Rindo?"

"I've found him honorable," Runyon said.

"Oh, Cal!" Her shock was genuine. "How can you say that?"

"Because I know it to be true," he said. "Bess, don't you see, we're fighting each other. I want to find a way out."

"What way is there?" she asked. "Cal, will you quit Rindo for me?"

"No," he said. "I've worked for the man too long." He picked up his hat and turned to the door. "What's going to happen to us, Bess? Were all the things we talked about just talk?"

A sudden whoop split the silence and a revolver popped. Bess looked quickly from the window, turning her head both ways. "They've got Ben!"

Whirling, she plunged past Cal Runyon. In the hallway she stopped and gave him a flat, uncompromising stare. "I guess we're already getting a taste of Cadmus Rindo's law."

"I'll go with you," he said quickly.

"I don't need you," she said. "I don't even want you around."

Then she was dashing for the head of the stairs; Runyon followed, then gave up the thought of chasing her.

The crowd on the street had migrated toward the jail. They were howling and discharging firearms into the air. One man was even trying to wedge a span of mules through Burkhauser's front door, while down the street, other mules were being hitched to logging dollies for an impromptu race through town. Bess Jamison hurried across the street, completely ignoring the traffic. One horseman cursed and pulled up short to keep from running her down, only to be plowed under by another who failed to stop in time.

Gaining the opposite boardwalk, Bess walked rapidly, but by the time she reached the corner, the crowd was breaking up and Ben Colfax was not in sight. At the jail door she knocked, for it was locked.

From inside, Ben Colfax said, "Who is it?"

"Bess."

He shot the bolt and let her in, then locked the door again. He had a handkerchief in one hand and was dabbing at a bleeding lip. A swelling over his eye was growing more pronounced by the minute. "I came close to killing men out there a few minutes ago," he said bleakly.

"No one could have blamed you," Bess said.

He shook his head and turned away so she could not see the shame in his expression. "I don't mind a licking, Bess, but the way I was licked hurts. Rindo thought so damned little of me that he ran a tramp against me. He had to rub my face in the dirt."

"It was a cruel thing," Bess said.

"The world's cruel," Ben Colfax said and sought comfort in a cigar. "Did you see how quick the wolves jumped me? A bunch of hired animals." He went around to the drawer side of his desk and lifted a ring of keys. "To think I had him in jail all the time," he said softly. "I'll sure have that rubbed in my face all right." He walked down the short hall to the cell blocks. Bess Jamison followed him.

The young man lay on his back, mouth open, snoring loudly. He needed a bath and shave and a lot more self-respect, Bess decided. Ben Colfax toed him without too much gentleness, nearly booting him off the bunk.

With a startled grunt, the young man opened his eyes and sat up. "Getting kind of heavy with your handling, ain't you?" He looked at Bess. "You the warden's daughter?"

"Keep a civil tongue in your head," Ben Colfax warned, "or I'll bat some sense into you."

Raising a hand, the young man touched a still tender bruise on his cheekbone. "Seems that you already did. You want to try again now that I'm sober?"

"You're free to go," Ben Colfax said. "I'll get your stuff."

He went back to his office. Bess leaned against the bars and studied Onart. Not a bad face, she decided. A little thin, but that was probably from drinking too much and skipping too many meals. Onart's hair was dark brown, straight as a string and badly in need of barbering. He had an oval face, without the heavy-boned ridges so common among thin men. His lips were long and thin, giving his expression a quality of cynicism that seemed somehow out of place.

He returned her stare for a moment, then said, "See anything you like, just ask for it. We carry it in stock."

"Smart, aren't you?" Bess tried to stare him down, but failed. She looked around the cell; a cot, washbasin and a cracked pitcher on the floor.

Ben Colfax tromped down the hall. He

had a shell belt draped over his arm and tossed it to Onart. "Now git!"

"You're in a hurry," Onart said easily. "I'm not." He turned the cartridge belt over and opened a small pocket on the back. Thrusting his fingers inside, he sounded it, then looked at Ben Colfax. "I see you found it. There was three hundred dollars in there."

"A likely story," Colfax said. He looked quickly at Bess. "They all try that. Claim you took their money." His attention whipped back to Onart. "Beat it, and if I hear you telling it around that I rolled you, I'll break your skull."

"I'll bet you will," Onart said. He smiled and lifted a booted foot to the bunk rail. Then he split open the sewed cuff of his trouser leg and palmed four twenty-dollar gold pieces. Ben Colfax' face darkened in sudden anger, and Onart's smile turned to a soft laugh. "Here's some you didn't get." Buckling on his gunbelt, Onart settled it on his hip, then expertly palmed the weapon and rotated the cylinder. "At least you didn't steal the shells," he said.

"Ben! Are you going to take that?" Bess Jamison placed her hands on her hips and glared at Onart.

"Call me a liar," Onart suggested. He motioned toward Bess, all the time looking at Ben Colfax. "Go on, tell her I'm making it up, that you don't roll every drunk."

Ben Colfax watched Onart, his expression drawn and hesitant. He looked at the gun Onart wore, and more especially, the way he wore it. Only a select breed of men wore a pistol like that, in a holster trimmed of all surplus leather and cut to ride so that the butt was always cocked away from the hip for easy access. And Ben had looked the gun over carefully while Onart slept in the cell. A gunsmith had plied his trade with cautious skill, hand-honing the lockwork until it was as smooth as butter. The original hammer had been altered and smoothed for slip-hammer shooting. Colfax' summation was that this was a money-making pistol, a for-hire pistol, and the man wearing it was better than most for he was still alive.

Glancing downcast at Bess, Colfax said, "The job never paid much, and a man slips into bad ways after awhile." He shifted his feet and moved his hands aimlessly. "Bess, you wouldn't hold this against old Ben, would you? It ain't like I'd ever been dishonest with anyone here. Just a few bums now and then."

"This isn't the time to discuss it," Bess Jamison said. She looked squarely at Onart. "Things have happened while you've been sleeping in jail."

Her glance toward Ben reminded him of the lost election and with considerable reluctance he unpinned the badge from his own vest and hooked it on the front of Onart's canvas jumper.

"What the hell's this?" Onart asked. "Some kind of joke?"

"We wish it were," Bess said, "but it's no joke. You've been elected sheriff."

The front door shook under a heavy fist and Ben went to open it; then the compounded step of several men came toward the cell block. They were all timber men with their multicolored wool shirts and calked boots that left torn dimples in the plank floor whenever they took a step. They looked at Onart, hard work and trouble blended in their expressions, revealing much of their lives to a single, observing glance.

Bess nodded at the leader. "Has everyone gone home, Jess?"

He pulled his attention away from Onart and looked at her. "Most of them are still hanging around, figuring maybe there was something you wanted to do." He made a curt motion toward Onart. "Is this what Rindo bought?"

"Who's Rindo?" Onart asked.

"The man who bought and paid for you,"

another man said. He was over six feet tall, shoulders as wide as a singletree, and his arms were sinewed boughs. This man touched Bess lightly. "You say it and I'll put a kink in this fella and take him back to Rindo."

"Let him," Ben Colfax suggested. "I'd like nothing better than to give some of this back to Rindo."

"It wouldn't be any trouble to me," the big man said, speaking softly. "What do you say, Bess?"

She pondered the question, her brow furrowed. To all appearances she was as collected as a housewife selecting the supper vegetables.

Onart said, "What kind of people are you anyway? The law picks a man's pockets and now you stand there talking about wrapping me up in a bundle to send to a man I don't even know."

"You don't mean a thing to us," Bess said flatly. "It's your tough luck this is happening, that's all."

Onart's glance touched each of them, then settled on the husky lumberjack. "You want to fight, is that it?"

"If Miss Jamison says so," the man admitted.

They were all watching Onart, but he had

drawn his gun before any of them could move. "Stand still," he said flatly, then edged out of the cell. He nodded his head toward Bess Jamison. "This bulldog of yours got a name?"

"Harry," she said.

"Come out here, Harry."

When the man stepped into the hall, Onart closed the cell door and turned the key. Ben Colfax grabbed the bars and shook them. "You got no call to lock us up!"

Onart laughed. "Fella, everyone in this town is crazy so I don't have to have a call to do anything. No more than you did to lift my money, or you," he looked at Bess, "to egg this ape on to mash in my head." He prodded the lumberjack in the small of the back with his gun. "Let's go to the front office where we'll have swinging room."

"Well now," Harry said, smiling. "I'll go for that."

Bess and Colfax were tugging at the cell door while the other two men stood back in silence. Onart urged the big man ahead of him, and, once in the office, took off his gunbelt and hung it on a handy peg. The rack of rifles on the wall was locked and Onart slipped his own gun into the middle desk drawer and locked it.

"Now we can make this nice and safe,"

Onart said.

Harry stripped off his shirt and laid it across the back of a chair. His chest was broad and flat, well thicketed with hair. When he stepped toward Onart, his calks left small blond tufts of pine on the floor.

"You mind locking the outer door?" Onart asked. "I wouldn't want you to run out when the going gets tough."

"No chance of that," Harry said. He turned the key and then tossed it into the corner. "You ready?"

"Sure," Onart said. "Let's get it started."

Harry's charge was as furious as a bull's. He plowed around the corner of the desk, all muscle and drive. Onart stepped away, swooped up the lamp and brought it down across the crown of the man's head. Shattered glass and kerosene flew in a wild spray, and Harry went to his knees with enough force to jar the building.

From the cell block, Bess yelled, "Harry! Harry, watch yourself!"

Onart walked around the far side of the desk and stood slightly behind the lumberjack as he pushed himself erect. There was an oozing split in his scalp. Before Harry could find Onart, the man doubled his fist and planted it in the soft spot behind Harry's ear.

Driven forward, Harry went asprawl across the desk, sliding to the floor on the other side. He landed head and shoulders first, dragged the rest of his long body around where it belonged, then looked at Onart. There was no anger in the lumberjack's eyes, just a new respect and a great deal of caution.

"You want to get up now?" Onart invited.

"I'll get up," the man said. "Just give me a minute."

"Why should I give you anything?" Onart asked, then swept forward, one foot swinging. He caught Harry as the man was trying to rise, and the boot arched him back. He landed flat on the floor, his mouth mashed. "We get rough now," Onart said and swept up a chair.

The down-swung furniture took the lumberjack across the head and shoulders as he was trying to roll. Driven flat, Harry pawed at the floor as though trying to find a purchase somewhere that wouldn't tip and rock.

Onart stepped back and waited, and when the man got enough strength to rise, he said, "One more, Harry," and picked up another chair. He waited until the man was on his feet, then stepped to one side and swung as though trying to cut down a tree. Some kindness prevented Onart from making a complete ruin of Harry's face; he struck him flush in the chest, catapulting him backward across the desk and into the wall.

Bess was shaking the cell door and demanding to know what was going on, so to bring her up to date, Onart half-dragged Harry down the short hall, unlocked the cell door, and pitched him in. Everyone looked at the big lumberjack, then at Onart.

Ben Colfax said it. "Who — are you, mister?"

"Now you ought to know me," Onart said softly. "You had me locked up for a week."

Ben Colfax raised a hand and pawed his mouth out of shape. "Don't get many of the real tough ones in this part of the country." He shook his head. "The name Onart don't mean anything to me, but I guess it should."

"Try the Wind River Kid and see what you get."

For an instant it looked as if Ben Colfax was going to strangle on his cigar; then he began to chuckle. This soon got out of control and he laughed. Finally he began to cry, all the time laughing in a high, half-hysterical voice. Bess took him by the arm and shook him. "What's so damned funny?"

With a supreme effort, Ben brought his mirth under control. He wiped the back of his hand across his eyes. "By God, that's poetic justice for you, Bess. Rindo elects a jailbird so he can get me out of office, then the man he elects turns out to be the Wind River Kid, as dangerous a man as Doc Holliday or Wes Hardin." He paused to suffer through a dying chuckle. "And I took his money, when all the time I could have got five hundred dollars for turning him over to an Arizona marshal."

"You're too greedy for your own good," the Kid said. He threw the cell door wide. "Go on, get out of here." He pointed to the tarnished sheriff's badge still pinned to his jumper. "Like it or not, this county's got itself a new sheriff."

Colfax left first, then Bess; she edged away from the Kid as though he would suddenly reach out and bite her. The two men who had come in with Harry helped him to his feet and outside. Bess stood by the front door while Colfax leaned against his desk. The Kid unlocked the middle drawer and rebuckled his gun. Colfax was looking around at the scattered destruction. Finally he said, "You could have hit him with the desk too, Kid."

"Didn't need to," the Kid said softly. "Harry wasn't as tough as he thought he was."

"Maybe you're not either," Bess said flatly.

"Lady," the Kid said, "why don't you get married and have kids?" He looked steadily at her, and then she went out, slamming the door. "What eats her?" he asked.

"She has her troubles," Colfax said. "We all do." He looked at the Wind River Kid. "This is logging country, Kid. What brings you here?"

"I need a change," the Kid said.

"Well," Colfax opined, "you got that all right. Never heard of you wearing a badge before." He got off the corner of the desk. "Too bad you had to come here, though. Rindo'll offer you some money and you'll take his orders. I know your kind, Kid. Hired out so long that it comes second nature."

"The same way you've picked so many pockets that you're no longer honest?"

This drove an angry color into Ben Colfax' face, but he kept a tight rein on himself. "You think what you want, Kid. At least the law ain't after me." He stepped to the door, pausing there. "The place is yours and you're welcome to it."

"Where can I find this man Rindo?"

"On the hotel porch if he ain't gone home. You want some advice?"

"From you?" The Wind River Kid shook

his head. "You need it worse than I do, mister."

"Suit yourself," Colfax said. "But you'd better get on the right side, Kid. The girl can use you with trouble coming on." He sighed. "She's a good sort, Kid. You got to forget that part in the cell. I don't guess Harry'll hold it against you either."

"I don't have to forget anything," the Kid said. "Go on, tend to your own business."

"All right," Ben Colfax said, "but I'll be around to watch you fall. Don't forget that you don't have a friend in this town. Bess's crowd would just as soon jump you as not, and once Rindo finds out who you are, he'll get rid of you. He's got a man fast enough to shade you too."

After Ben Colfax closed the door, the Wind River Kid sat down behind the desk and tried to adjust his thinking to this new turn of affairs. With eight hundred miles between himself and his stomping ground, any man would consider himself safe, but evidently this was a miscalculation; he certainly had fallen into the exact thing he wished to avoid.

Strange, he thought, that a man of twenty-four could consider his life drawing to a close, or at least the major run of it behind him. That kind of thinking can drive a man across many a weary mile, and in the end desert him, leaving him exactly as he had been, only just a little older and much more tired.

The Kid mentally recounted his two-week spree in Rindo's Springs and was sorry that he'd ever bought that first bottle; whiskey had never liked him and after a good drunk he liked it even less than before.

Leaving the office, he walked slowly along the main street, breathing in the rich odors of pitch and burning slabs from the giant incinerator. A small crowd cluttered the porch of Burkhauser's Saloon and the Kid gave them a careful look before he entered. He wondered if Ben Colfax had spread the word about his identity, then decided that the ex-sheriff would keep still; he wanted others to share his surprise. Probably make him feel less of a damned fool that way.

Ben Colfax was leaning against the bar, and around him were several men, all loggers and none his friends — the Kid could tell by the way they left Colfax standing by himself. The aroma of spilled beer and old cigars whetted a thirst in the Kid and he bellied up to the bar. One of the men turned and gave him a brass-faced stare, his glance lingering on the tarnished badge.

"So you're what Rindo bought?" The man

chuckled.

The bartender was waiting, either for the Kid's order or a signal to duck. "Draw a beer," the Kid said; then while the tap sizzled, he glanced at the man. "How much did it cost you, mister?"

"Not a nickle."

"Then keep your mouth shut about how other people spend their money," the Kid said. He had a manner of speaking, in a near whisper, that made men cock their ears and listen. It was almost as though he were determined never to shout or speak up, or repeat what he had said, and because men were afraid they would miss something important, they listened most carefully.

The man next to the Kid stiffened slightly. He was tall and stringy and as tough as the rock hills. No logger, this man. The Kid felt a chord of recognition strike, then he remembered him from Kansas, a gunman, and far from second-rate.

Of course there would be one in Rindo's Springs; there seemed to be one in every town, just waiting for trouble. He tried to recall the man's name, then he had it: Pete Davis. Fragments of the man's achievements came to him, the men he had killed in the course of a brief and frantic career. The Kid knew without thinking that here was a bit of business that would have to be taken care of sooner or later, whether he liked it or not.

Farther down the bar, Cal Runyon shifted his weight and said, "Ease off, Pete. The old man don't pay you to shoot off your mouth."

The Kid looked past Pete Davis and locked eyes with Cal Runyon. "You somebody important?"

"Not really," Runyon said. He picked up his beer and came around the cluster of men, edging in between the Kid and Davis. "I work for Cadmus Rindo, the man who elected you."

The Kid never took his attention from either man. Both seemed to be unarmed, but he wasn't sure. Pete used to carry his gun in a half-breed spring rig under his coat, and that had never slowed him down. The Kid lifted his beer, drank, then set the stein aside. He said, "And where can I find the kind old soul who goes around making sheriffs out of strangers?"

Cal Runyon nodded toward the street. "At the hotel, most likely." He pursed his lips and rolled a thought around in his mind. "You sound sore. Better get over it. There's nothing to be sore about."

"Sounds reasonable," the Kid said. He

took another swallow of beer, then turned away from the bar. At the door he said, "That was on you, wasn't it?"

Runyon smiled faintly. "You got any other name besides Onart?"

So Ben Colfax hadn't told. . . . "Ask Pete, he knows me," the Kid said and stepped outside. Across the street and a few doors down sat the hotel, and as he walked along, the Kid studied the building carefully. On the upper gallery he saw a man sitting in a wheelchair, a heavy robe over his legs. On the lower gallery he saw another man and knew without asking that this was Cadmus Rindo. The old man followed him with his eyes, and at the barbershop the Kid paused to look back. He saw Pete Davis leave the saloon and cross over to where Cadmus Rindo sat. There was a hurried conference; then the Kid turned his back on it and went into the barbershop.

Leaning back in the chair, he indicated that he wanted a shave and a haircut and damn little conversation. The barbershop was warm and spiced with the fragrance of shaving lotions, and the barber was a skilled man.

After the shave and haircut I ought to get out, the Kid thought. After I take care of Pete, he told himself, then realized that this was the way it had always been: pushing on, but only after he had taken care of the business at hand. Although he never thought much about it, he was always a little amazed at himself for being able to anticipate trouble before it loomed. But he knew that Pete's attitude had warned him. And the way he had eased off at Cal Runyon's order clearly indicated that he was willing to wait. Add it up and it spelled trouble, but that was the Wind River Kid's business, a business in which he handled himself well.

There was not much left of the day when he stepped out on the boardwalk. A gray dusk was settling, building sooty shadows along one side of the street. At the lumber camp, the whistle was shrilling and the ring of gang saws began to tone down in pitch as they were slowed down and shut off.

By some unvoiced call, many people began to form in ranks along the boardwalks, making an unsuccessful attempt to look casually idle.

Pete Davis was standing near the hotel entrance, his hands thrust into his coat pockets. Cal Runyon was on the saloon porch with Ben Colfax, while old man Rindo still sat in his rocking chair, his eyes never leaving the Wind River Kid.

Then Pete decided to cross the street

toward the saloon, but he stopped in the middle for another look toward the barbershop. When he saw he was being watched, he bent, picked up a rock, then casually flung it through the butcher's plate glass window. The glass cascaded over the boardwalk, and the butcher ran out, cleaver in hand, shouting dire threats. Then he saw Pete standing there and the anger melted. Mumbling, he backed into his store again and closed the door.

For an instant longer, the Kid just watched; then when Pete looked at him and grinned, the Kid started down the walk toward the saloon. And as he walked he asked himself why he cared. There was more here to aggravate him than Pete's smug smile. He'd run into this before — the feeling a town had when one man had it by the throat and wouldn't let go. Then came the question: Why did he have to do anything about it? Other men saw the same thing and only shrugged and rode on their way, but he couldn't do that. Some basic chemistry in him revolted and he had another fight on his hands.

He stepped onto Burkhauser's porch and went inside. A crowd was waiting. Pete was leaning against the bar, a beer in his hand. His glance was full on the Kid when he stepped up. Pete said, "You gettin' thirsty again, Drunk?"

There was no change at all in the Kid's expression. "I could go for a beer." A waggling finger stirred the bartender to his taps. When the Kid had the beer, he added, "Pretty good throwing arm you got there."

"You saw that, huh? Always wanted to break a window."

"Well you sure did that one," the Kid said. He drank some of his beer. "Now let's go pay the butcher what it'll cost to replace it."

The Kid's voice had been so deceptively soft that Pete couldn't believe he had been serious. He stared for an instant, then tipped his head back to laugh.

His mouth came open, but the sound died in his throat, for the Kid planted a rock-hard fist against the point of his jaw. Pete spun back against the bar, arms outflung, and the Kid caught him as he began to sag.

"Give me a bucket of water," he said to the bartender.

"Nothing here but the slop bucket," the man said.

"Hell, that's good enough for him. Hand it over." The bartender hesitated, then hoisted a wooden bucket. The Kid heaved the suds into Pete's face, bringing him around at least to the point where he could partially support himself. Every man in that saloon held his breath and watched as though he were deathly afraid of missing something. Many of the men were timber workers on Cadmus Rindo's payroll, but the Kid counted on their minding their own business, and he was not mistaken.

Pete was clinging to the bar, nearly unconscious. The Kid said, "Now let's go pay for that window. I asked you nice but you were too thick-headed to hear. I won't tell you again."

He fisted a handful of Pete's collar and flung him toward the swinging doors. Pete banged against them just as another man was coming up on the other side, and the impact sent this man sprawling and cursing across the porch while Pete clung to the louvered panels for support. When the Kid came up behind him, Pete tried to whirl and make a fight of it, but another hard fist in his mouth propelled him backward across the porch, his boots scraping for purchase. His heels caught and he spilled down the short steps to the street below.

The Kid took his time, and when Pete got groggily to his feet, the Kid was behind him, pushing him with stiffened arms.

A throng of interested spectators followed the two men as they headed for the butcher's shop. The butcher came to his doorway, a heavy man with worry in his dark eyes. He wiped his hands nervously on his blood-stained apron. When his glance touched Pete, there was a hint of apology in it, as though he were sorry the man was being put to this trouble simply because he broke a window.

The Kid gave Pete a final push and stopped before the butcher. He asked, "How much is it going to cost to replace the window?"

The butcher looked at Pete, then at Pete's friends, who made up a bulk of the crowd. He grinned but it turned off sickly. "I guess it was all in fun, so I'll replace it myself."

"I asked you how much?" The Kid's voice was soft and easy and even the butcher understood that this man was making a concession — he didn't often repeat himself.

Pete raised his bloody head and looked squarely at the butcher. "Be careful now, Donegan. He caught me off guard. I'll use my gun the next time."

This was hint enough. The butcher spread his hands in an appeal for sympathy, under-standing. "I don't want any trouble, fella. Let's just let this go."

"You had trouble when the rock came through the window," the Kid pointed out.

"Are you going to make out a complaint?"

"Complaint? Christ no! I've got to do business with these men."

Pete's manner became suddenly assured, even arrogant. He looked around at the crowd and laughed. "Well, Tin-star, you seem to have sunk an ax into more'n you can chop."

"A law's been broken," the Wind River Kid said. "If it ain't on the books, then it ought to be. Now pay for the window."

"He said —"

"I don't give a damn what he said!" the Kid suddenly fisted Pete's shirt front, jerked him off balance, slapped him twice across the face, then gave him a backward shove. He crowded against Pete, his hands slapping pockets until he found the hardness of metal coins. Then the Kid ripped the cloth, scattering money on the floor. "Pick up ten dollars," the Kid said, "and pay the butcher."

There was a hesitation, then Ben Colfax, who stood on the boardwalk, spoke up in a voice that could be heard the length of the street. "That's the new law, boys — the Wind River Kid!"

To many, the name meant nothing, but to a few it spelled trouble. Pete, who had his pride and reputation to think of, looked quickly at the Kid, then bent down and retrieved ten dollars. He thrust the money at the butcher and started to move away.

The Kid took him by the arm and hauled him back. "Get something through your head, Davis. You thought you had a big thing here with the butcher too scared to complain, but the law was still broken, and if I have to, I'll do the complaining for those too timid to do for themselves. I don't give a damn if you break every window in this town, but if you do you'll pay for every one. Not because it's the law, but because it's justice. I know your reputation, but it don't scare me."

Pete waited an additional moment. "You through talking?" He stepped back, out of the Kid's reach. "You can bet I'll see you again soon. With a gun."

"You're smarter than that," the Kid said flatly.

For another moment Pete lingered, at least long enough to convince the onlookers that he wasn't exactly running. Then he wheeled and began to batter his way through the crowd. The Kid stood by the door until the butcher went inside and the crowd began to melt a little around the outer edges. As the boardwalk cleared he noticed a young woman standing there, pencil and notebook in her hand. She looked quite intense, giving him her undivided attention. Ben Colfax was still on the boardwalk and he edged over until he stood close to the young woman. He said, "You axed yourself quite a swath, Kid. He'll get you for that."

Though he had intended to turn away, the Kid pivoted on his heel and came over. He looked more carefully at the girl and she met his eyes frankly. She was younger than he had at first thought, not more than twenty. Her pale hair was wavy and unfettered, falling well past her shoulders.

The Wind River Kid realized that he was staring and pulled his eyes away. To Colfax, he said, "Got any tobacco?" When the sack was passed over, he gave his attention to the manufacture of a cigaret.

"I'd never have tackled Pete Davis," Colfax said gently. "You were lucky he didn't have his gun on. But you can bet he won't go without it from now on."

"Be something to look forward to, huh?"

This made Colfax pause. Then he said, "I learned something about you tonight, Kid. You don't hesitate to jump a man. Most men shy away from Pete's kind. Even when a fight's buildin', they wait 'til the last minute before swinging. But you're different. I'd say you're most eager to meet trouble more'n halfway." He tapped the Kid on the arm, drawing his attention around. "Take a look across the street. There's another man who don't duck trouble."

The Kid turned and, across the brief interval of the street, met the blunt, uncompromising stare of Cadmus Rindo. The man's glance had weight to it, and an open challenge, which was accepted in silence by the Kid.

Finally Rindo heaved himself erect, made a hand motion to a man down the street, then waited there, stony-faced, until his buggy was brought up. He mounted and lifted the reins, wheeling about to stop in front of the new sheriff.

Cadmus Rindo's voice was a soft bass rumble when he spoke. "There was a time when a drunk could be counted on to be nothing more than a drunk."

"Times must have changed," the Kid said easily.

"What are you doing in this part of the country?" Rindo asked. "This is timber. Guns and cattle are a thousand miles south."

"A man gets tired of one thing all the time," the Kid told him.

Rindo grunted and fingered his flowing mustache. "And it was my luck to pick you."

He lifted the reins. "But I guess it's a mistake I can correct easy enough. Be gone from this town in the morning."

He drove off down the street and turned out of sight at the next corner.

2

Cadmus Rindo's ultimatum and departure left a wake of silence, but Ben Colfax broke it when he said, "The old man wasn't fooling."

"I didn't think he was," the Kid said.

"You ought to have let Pete Davis have his fun," Colfax said. "Rindo put him up to that to see what you'd do."

"And he found out," the Kid said. He looked carefully at Ben Colfax. "You don't see what I'm getting at, do you?"

"Can't say as I do," Colfax admitted. He looked at the young woman who stood slightly to the rear of the Kid. "You, Nan?"

"Yes," she said quietly. "I see it."

"Then somebody tell me," Colfax suggested.

"The law was broken," the Kid said. "It wouldn't matter to me whose man broke it, or whether he was fast with a gun."

Ben Colfax cuffed his hat forward over his

eyes and scratched his head. "That sounds darn funny coming from you," he said. "There's an Arizona warrant out for you. In any other town you'd be just another Pete Davis."

"That warrant's not for breaking the law," the Kid said.

Shaking his head, Ben Colfax turned and shuffled down the street. The Kid followed him with his eyes for a moment, then turned toward the jail.

"May I walk with you?" the young woman asked.

"Any reason you should?"

"I think so," she said and waited. Finally he shrugged and they turned down the boardwalk together. At the jail he went in ahead of her and put a match to the lamps.

"Close the door," he said, and began building a small fire to ward off the night chill. A few sweeps with his booted foot pushed the shattered chairs into one corner and he drew up the remaining one. "Care to sit down?"

"Thank you," she said. She straightened the folds of her dress and held her pad and pencil in her lap.

He glanced at them, then said, "You a writer?"

She seemed startled. "Oh! I'm Nan Buckley. I run the newspaper."

He went to the stove to shake it down and adjust the damper, for a good blaze was crackling and the cast iron belly was shedding heat into the room. "You think I'm good for a story?"

"Perhaps," she said. "If I can understand why you're so angry."

He raised his eyes and looked quickly at her. The lamplight made her face seem more full, yet the blandness of artificial light could not detract from her radiant complexion. Her eyes were blue; he had been sure they would be. And her lips were full and firm, mirroring her changing moods. They were evenly compressed in this moment of seriousness, and the Kid felt an almost overwhelming desire to see them smile.

"Am I angry?" he asked evenly.

"Very angry," she said. "They could well call you the Angry Man, instead of the Wind River Kid."

"You've got quite an imagination," the Kid said.

Nan Buckley shook her head. "I think not. You were angry when you came to Rindo's Springs. Very angry at yourself, because you tried to drink Burkhauser's place dry the first night. And I understand that you were quarrelsome, and over nothing at all." She paused. "Tell me why you're so angry."

"So you can put it in the paper?" He gathered up the smashed furniture and chucked the pieces into the stove, then closed the door with his foot.

"We don't put everything in the paper," Nan said. "Don't you want help at all, Mr. — ah —"

"Kid," he said. "It's as good a name as any." After digging through the desk drawer, he found a cigar and spent a moment lighting it. Then he planted his elbows solidly on the pine desktop and regarded her through a veil of smoke. His eyes seemed without humor, yet there was a capacity for laughter in them. Finally he said, "You're looking at a man who's worn out. Used up." He smiled and fanned smoke aside. "You ever been tired? Not the kind you can cure with sleep, but bone tired. Tired of living from day to day. Tired of being with the same kind of people all the time." He shook his head. "You wouldn't know the kind I mean. The ones that buy everything, especially unpleasant things."

"There's unpleasantness here in Rindo's Springs," she said. "Are you angry because you ran into the very thing you wished to escape?"

He thought about this, then pursed his

lips. "Partly, I suppose." He let the cigar rest idly between his thumb and forefinger. "You know about me? About the Wind River Kid?"

"You're a gunfighter," she said. "Some say you're bad and there's a reward out for you."

He chuckled at her simplified answer. "Do you know what you're talking about?"

"No," she said. "But I want to know. Why did you come here?"

"An accident," he said. "No one sent for me, if that's what you're thinking. I don't hire out anymore like Pete Davis."

"I wasn't thinking that. But this isn't your kind of country, or your kind of men." She raised a hand slightly, half apologetically. "I'm not trying to belittle you, but this is logging country. You won't understand us, and we don't understand you." Her fingers plucked idly at a loose thread on the front of her dress. "You're in a strange position, the victim of an old man's angry prank that somehow backfired in his face."

The Wind River Kid touched the tarnished badge. "Is this genuine?"

"Yes," Nan admitted. "The election was legal. Cadmus Rindo merely put on some additional men at his mill. Enough to sway the election his way."

"You make it sound like I ought to resign," the Kid said.

"I'm sure I didn't mean it that way. But I'd do anything I could for this town. It's worth saving, even if it meant encouraging you to get Pete Davis into a gunfight and kill him."

"What's in this town that's worth saving?" the Kid asked flatly.

She smiled. "You're a man without a home; you wouldn't have said that otherwise." Then she paused, gaining a slight insight into this man. "Perhaps that's part of your anger. You need a home desperately and can't find one."

His first impulse was to deny this loudly, but he did not. Lifting his cigar, he found that it had gone out, and he rekindled it before speaking. "Being run out of towns gets tiresome. After a man gets a reputation, folks won't take a chance on him." He shrugged. "I had big ideas. Told myself that the only way to get out was to get way out, into a country that hadn't seen my kind and wouldn't recognize it if they did. That was a foolish hope. A man's a damn cow, carrying his brand wherever he goes."

"You're impatient," she said. "If you worked as hard at starting anew as you did to build your reputation —" She stopped speaking and stood up. "Well, it's none of my business what you do."

"It seems that you're making it your business," he said. "What kind of an ax are you grinding on my backside?"

A faint smile lifted her lips and a new sparkle came into her eyes. "I think you might be good for Rindo's Springs. I'd like to suggest something, if I may."

"Go ahead. You will anyway."

"I'd like to write about you in my paper." He frowned, but she ignored it. "Like a word portrait. After all, you're the new sheriff, and people have a right to know what kind of a man they have behind the law." She paused to study him. "There are going to be a lot of lies circulated about you. The best way to stop that is to tell the facts."

"What does this get me?" he asked.

"Nothing," she said, "but it might help Rindo's Springs."

He mulled this over in his mind for a time. "A list of my activities isn't going to read like an alderman's report. Most of it I'd as soon not talk about."

"Then you choose to hide the facts?" Nan asked. "Kid, you want people to accept you, but what do you intend to give them in return? A dubious past? A closed mouth when anyone asks you anything? Anger at them for not understanding something you won't allow them to understand?" She turned to the door. "I was mistaken; I can't help you at all."

"Wait," he said, coming around the desk. "There's an Arizona warrant out for me. If the word got back there —"

"I understand perfectly," she said smoothly. "Kid, one of these days you're going to find out that you can't hide. And once a thing is out in the open, it never is as bad as you imagined it." She picked up his hat and handed it to him. "This is your chance. Are you going to let the people of Rindo's Springs know what kind of a man they have in office or not?"

She waited while he thought about it, and he remembered the other towns he had found that he liked, and left as soon as someone identified him. Moving on could get to be a habit with a man, a bad habit. Then too, this woman had a persuasive manner. He smiled and said, "We'll try it your way, as long as it's painless."

She placed a hand flat against his chest. "Wait. I didn't say it was painless. I just said it wouldn't be as bad as you imagined."

His eyes traveled over her features carefully as though he might find a clue to her thoughts there. "What are you trying to do, reform me?"

"Do you need it?" Her smile lurked in her eyes. She opened the door and waited while he turned down the lamps. He locked the office and pocketed the key; then they turned down the street together. The town was quiet for all the business houses were closed, except for Burkhauser's place, which held a lively crowd. The air was moist and heavy and the acrid smoke from burning wood was almost overpowering. When they drew abreast of the saloon, the Kid became aware of Murray Burkhauser standing in the blackest shadows. The saloon keeper's cigar glowed darkly red, then faded.

"You look like you're in a hurry," Burkhauser said. "Got a minute?"

They stopped. Nan said, "I'll go on ahead and put on a pot of coffee. You can't miss the place. Second side street."

"All right," the Kid said and watched her move away. When she was out of earshot, he turned to Burkhauser. "Make it fast."

"You've got time for one on the house, haven't you? No?" He shrugged. "Ben Colfax timed that pretty good when he identified you tonight." Burkhauser bent forward as if to make a closer examination. "I expected you to be an older man, if you can judge by the stories." His glance touched the Kid's gun. "Something a little fancier there. Pearl handles, maybe, or a twin on the other hip."

"If you've got something to say," the Kid said, "suppose you get to it."

"All right," Burkhauser said. He cast his cigar into the street where it died in a shower of sparks. "You plan to stay on in Rindo's Springs, or are you going to treat the election as the joke that it is and leave?"

"No joke to me."

Burkhauser frowned. "Kid, this is no place for you. What's in it for you?"

"There doesn't have to be anything in it," the Kid said. "A lot of times there isn't a thing you can put in your pocket."

"You and I differ there," Burkhauser stated. "I like to put things in my pockets. This town has sides, Kid. Better pick one and stick with it."

"Which side are you on?"

"I'm on my own," Burkhauser admitted. "You hate money?"

"No, I get along all right with it. But it's not a disease with me."

Burkhauser chuckled. "You're looking at a man who's afflicted. I'm not alone. The old man, Cadmus Rindo, owns everything around here. It's his town, his bank, and his money in it." He moved his hands in a small circle. "But there's always competition. Bess Jamison's outfit cramps the old man. He'd be happier if she was in some other business besides logging." Burkhauser stepped down and tapped the Wind River Kid on the chest. "This town is made up of the 'haves' and 'have nots'." He paused to smile slyly. "Then there are a few who try to pinch a little from each."

"And that's you," the Kid said.

"I do what I can," he said. "This saloon is mine, and I have a little money spread around where it'll do the most good. But Rindo's the key timber here. Get him and everything will fall down because he holds everything up. You're a smart man, Kid. You rode into this town with a yen to see new places. All right, you've seen them. Now ride on out and let Bess Jamison and Rindo fight. Let everything collapse of its own accord."

"While you pick up the pieces?"

Burkhauser shrugged. "No harm in that." He patted his inner coat pocket. "You could leave about four hundred dollars richer, Kid."

"That's a lot of money," the Kid said. "I'll think about it."

"But not too long," Burkhauser cautioned.

"Come and see me in the morning before you leave."

Burkhauser turned then and walked into his saloon. The Kid stood there for a brief interval, then went on down the street. A resentment began to simmer, for few men are flattered when other men offer to buy them; yet this had happened before and he had always managed to pass it off. But somehow this was different, a little more insulting. Perhaps because he had mentally shed his old habits.

He found the newspaper office; gilt letters on the glass paneled door identified *The Rindo County Free Press.* The Kid knocked and almost immediately Nan Buckley came to the door. She did not light a lamp in the front of the shop, but led him through the gloom to the office and living quarters she kept in the back.

"Did Murray try to buy you off?"

"Yes," he said, surprised. "You know him pretty well."

"I know everyone in Rindo's Springs," she said. "All their secrets." She motioned toward a chair. "Want some coffee?"

"Thanks, yes." He sat down and looked around the room. There was a well-worn comfort about everything, the furniture, the flowered rug on the floor, and the curtains over the rear windows. Much of this woman's personality was revealed in the room.

He studied her as she poured the coffee — a graceful woman with a composed face, as though all her troubles were minor ones. After handing him the cup, she took a seat across from him; her hands rested in her lap and she reminded him of a schoolgirl waiting for her first beau.

"You think it's strange, being here in my parlor, don't you?"

"I thought that, yes." He smiled. "I even wonder why I'm here."

"You're a smart man," she said. "Smart enough to realize that this has to be the last town. The Wind River Kid has run himself to the ground."

That she could pin this down so precisely amazed him; then a good reason occurred to him. "You've seen this happen before?"

"Yes," she said. "My father. He ran. He just couldn't stop and admit that he left mistakes behind." She bent forward slightly and her tone became intense. "Please, do this for yourself, no one else. Stay in Rindo's Springs." Then she relaxed, her expression again composed. "This is not like most towns. Here one man owns everything. You saw how it was with Pete Davis and the broken window; all of them were afraid to object. Most people here are like that, afraid. But you're not. The Wind River Kid doesn't owe Cadmus Rindo a cent. The only obligation you have is to yourself. That's why I believe you will be good for this town." She looked squarely at him. "Is this warrant serious?"

"I was in the Chino Valley War," he said. "Is that serious enough?"

"I'm going to print that," Nan Buckley stated. "I'm going through the old files and dig up everything I can that's fact and print it."

"That'll call the dogs quick enough," the Kid said. "For the life of me, I can't decide what you're after." He paused to sip his coffee before it got cold. "A man like me tries to bury everything and you seem determined to dig it out. Besides, I don't know as I like this town. What's to stop me from leaving?"

"Nothing," she said, "unless you want to admit I'm right."

"About there being an end to how far a man can run?" He laughed and set his coffee cup aside. "Paint me any color you want, and I'm still the Wind River Kid. That's something that won't rub off until I'm dead."

He got up, picked his hat off a small table

and walked toward the door. She followed him through the dark shop. "I wanted you to stay so badly," she said. "You are leaving, aren't you?"

"Good night, Miss Buckley," he said and walked back to the jail.

He unlocked the door, then turned the key after he closed it. The lamp still shed a feeble glow into the room and he took it with him into the small ell-shaped sleeping room off the hall. There he settled on the bunk, his hands clasped behind his head.

Most men, he knew, were forty or fifty before they had any genuine regrets, but here he was, twenty-five and wishing he could wipe it all out, forget that anything wrong had ever happened. It's hell, he conceded, to be half an outlaw. He supposed that was what he deserved for tagging along on the fringes of the really tough ones. Still, he could never take a lawless life too seriously; some deep sense of decency had always pulled him clear before the mud got too high on his boots. There had been some shooting from time to time, but a man could hardly be condemned because he was fast with a gun. Besides, the law had called this self-defense, since the others had drawn first.

Still this left an evil tang in the Kid's

mind. Every time he rode into a town, the sheriff would advise him to ride on. No one, it seemed, wanted trouble, yet it clung to him like beggar lice.

Joining that Chino Valley bunch had been a fool stunt; he realized it now. Still, the pay had been good, or so it had seemed at the time. A man couldn't look into the future, he decided. How was he to know that warrants would be sworn out against the losing faction? Just another shove to keep him moving, make him like Pete Davis, a real trouble-hunter.

Putting the past aside, he understood that he had no real business in Rindo's Springs. The badge he wore was, as Murray Burkhauser said, an old man's joke, or revenge against Ben Colfax. The Wind River Kid had no right to wear such an emblem of authority.

His talk with Nan Buckley disturbed him more than he cared to admit. She was right; he had gone about as far as a man could go when he had no distinct destination. Yet he could not stay. She was, above all things, an honest woman, and when her paper came out, the Wind River Kid would be known to all; he believed her when she said she would dig up the facts. He was, he supposed, in the position of the man who had never objected to having his hair ruffled, but was angered when someone disturbed the toupee that concealed his baldness. All men accumulated some bad things during the run of their lives, and even voiced no objection when called bad. But no man liked to have his sins listed in print.

Rising from the bunk, the Kid walked into the main office, set the lamp on the desk, then placed the tarnished badge beside it. Looking at this piece of metal, he felt a genuine regret. Under different circumstances he might have worn it with pride.

The town was asleep when he stepped to the boardwalk. Burkhauser's place was still alive, but then most saloons were nocturnal. He walked toward the stable near the end of the street, and in the coal darkness, searched out and saddled his horse. He supposed that Nan Buckley would miss him briefly, but since he really meant nothing to her, she would soon forget that the Wind River Kid had passed through.

He still had a few dollars, his gun, and enough shells. That should get him to San Francisco. Lively town, or so he had heard. With this thought in mind, he turned out of town and took the west road.

3

Bess Jamison's place was in the high timber nearly eight miles northwest of Rindo's Springs, and being a conservative woman who knew the value of a dollar, she chose not to rent a room at the hotel; instead she drove back to her home. The road was little more than a rutted logging trail, and as she wound up the dark slope, thunder rumbled and reverberated through the mountains. Lightning flashed whitely, revealing the timber in brief, ghostly light. When the rain began, she stopped and put up the top to her buggy, then drove on.

Her camp nestled in a short valley, and there were only a few lights glowing in the bunkhouse when she drove across the muddy yard. She was putting up her team in the barn when a man splashed across, stepping high to keep out of the deeper puddles. When he came to the barn door, Bess said, "Go back to bed, Henry. There won't be any work tomorrow."

She went on to the house, half-running in the rain. On the porch she paused to whip the water from her hair and face. Once inside, she stoked the fire in the back room, pulled the shades, then stripped completely and stood before the stove, toasting first on one side, then the other. When the heat had soaked into her, she padded in her bare feet, ladling grounds into the coffee pot. The flickering fire cast glowing lights on her bare flesh, building deep shadows around the smooth curves of her body.

While the coffee boiled she took a towel and dried her hair, then her legs, for the whipping rain had saturated her clothes to the waist. While she dried off, she heard a horseman approach the house. Walking into the other room, she took a robe from a closet and slipped into it as knuckles rattled the door.

"Come in," she called and tied the robe tightly. She held the loose edge to keep it from exposing her legs when she walked.

Ben Colfax stepped quickly inside, beating water from his hat. He took off his poncho and hung it dripping on the hall tree. "Oregon weather," he said sourly, his hands patting his pockets for a cigar. Then he tipped his head back and keened the air.

"That coffee I smell?"

"Come into the kitchen," Bess said. She took cups and saucers from the pine cupboard and placed them on the table. "Late for you to be out, Ben. And it's a long ride from town."

"You left too early," he said, then told her about the Kid's run-in with Pete Davis. "Of course Pete'll kill him for it, but not until he's had his fun making him sweat."

Bess listened carefully, pouring the coffee while he talked. Then she sat down across from him, her forearms flat on the table. "It looks like Rindo can't control his own sheriff," she said.

"Well," Ben said, scratching his head, "being the Wind River Kid, he's a little hard to control. The way I hear it, a man could get shot for trying to lean on the Kid when he wasn't in the mood for it."

"Then if he's against Rindo, we need him," Bess said.

Ben Colfax sipped his coffee slowly, pausing now and then to pour some into the saucer to cool it. "Bess, he don't have to be against anything." He reached across the table and patted her hand. "I guess you made a mistake, invitin' Harry to rough him up. This kid can handle himself, fists or guns. Rindo found that out too, and he's ordered the Kid out of town."

"Do you think he'll go?" Bess Jamison asked.

Colfax' shoulders rose and fell. "A man of his reputation hates to be told to do anything. Likely he's made up his mind to stay. He could be a help to you, Bess, was you to play the cards right."

"Tell me how, Ben."

He pursed his lips and fingered his mustache. "Seein' as how I'm no longer the law and don't have to be neutral, I guess I could offer a little advice. No man can work and fight at the same time, Bess. If Rindo and the Kid got to squabblin', the old man might get so busy he'd forget to tend to business." Colfax leaned back in the chair, one arm hooked over the edge behind him. "Your daddy must have been pressin' Rindo pretty hard, to get killed sudden like he did. I still ain't satisfied with Rindo's story. Too pat. Too thin." He got up and went to the stove for a refill on his coffee. " 'Course, Cal Runyon's testimony turned the trick for Rindo. That never satisfied me, either. Cal's a company man, through and through. You know that."

"Yes," she said softly. "And he'll never change, Ben. I've given up hoping."

He came over and stood behind her chair,

looking down at her. "Bess, you want to stay small? You want to go on payin' Rindo for the use of his mill? Go on shippin' over his railroad?" He leaned forward and put his hands on her shoulders. "There are merchants in town who want out. You're not alone, Bess. There's all the help you'll ever need, providin' the Kid don't side with the old man. And it looks like he's playing a lone hand, lightin' into Pete the way he did."

"We've got to be sure," she said. "Ben, when we buy chips into this, everything goes on the board, win or lose. I don't want to bet too early. Not until I know who's playing." She fell silent for a time, then when she spoke, her voice was hard. "Pa died because he wouldn't knuckle under to Rindo. I'll never forget that."

"That's the ticket," Colfax said. He came around to his own chair and sat down. "If you need any more money —"

She held up her hand and shook her head. "I'm already deep in your debt, Ben." Her smile was gentle. "I don't know what I'd have done without you. Lost everything, probably. I want to own this land, Ben. I want to own it free and clear, not work it for Cadmus Rindo."

"Well, it ain't as if he's takin' a tithing," Ben said. "He gave your pa permission to

71

log it off."

"It's not the same," she said flatly. "Ben, I'm not the kind who can live by another man's grace. Every time I see Rindo I think that all he'd have to do to get rid of me would be to kick me off with a court order. As long as I'm living like this, I have that threat over me."

"The world's a tough place to live," Ben Colfax said, rising. "Somehow, a man never gets so high he's free of other men. Rindo was here first and put his mark on the country. Ain't hardly a man here that he didn't give something to."

"Give?" She laughed derisively. "Just loaned, Ben. That's all."

"It gets kind of tiresome arguin'," he said and walked to the door. She followed him. The rain still fell heavily, rippling off the eaves, turning the yard into a bed of mud. Ben wiped his hand over the saddle, planing off most of the water before mounting. "If I see Cal Runyon," he said, "is there anything I should say?"

"Tell him I don't want him hurt," Bess said. "No, don't tell him that. We've said everything that's to be said."

"All right," he said. "Good night, Bess."

He turned his horse and rode back toward town. People, he had to admit, were generally a bunch of fools, not satisfied with what they had. Forty years before, give or take a season, Cadmus Rindo had struck the first ax blow to this country, and within ten years, had carved out a town, and then given it away, building by building. His strength and hard-headedness had built an industry, and a railroad, and incurred more enemies than any man had a right to have.

Of course, Colfax decided, the rest followed as sure as the sun. Men came and looked and wanted, and all the pleasantness vanished while a man's accomplishment became a stone weighing him down, making him struggle to keep what he had built. An old story to Ben Colfax, who had been seeing it or hearing it in one form or another all his life. And a goodly portion of that time had been spent trying to walk the neutral path down the center.

Colfax rode head down, letting the drizzling rain pour off his hat. He was quite surprised when his horse stopped, snorting and quivering. He stood in the stirrups, trying to penetrate the ink shadows. Then suddenly a horseman loomed close, but instead of stopping, spurred past and raced on.

Turning in the road, Colfax yelled and started after the rider, then quickly gave up the idea. He sat in silence, hearing only the prattle of rain which swallowed all other sounds. Finally he rounded his horse and went on toward Rindo's Springs.

The street was dark and empty when he arrived. He rode straight through to the lumber company offices at the far end of town. A guard stepped out of the shadows near the closed gate, his shotgun poised. Then he recognized Colfax and relaxed slightly.

"Cal Runyon around?" Colfax asked.

"There's still a light in his office," the guard said. "Go on in."

The gate was opened and Colfax eased his horse through. He was in Cadmus Rindo's empire now. Around him stood the sheds and machinery which ground out vast quantities of plank and stumping and railroad ties. A huge wagon park sat on the right with several, huge-wheeled logging arches arrayed behind that. Farther off was the mule corral, covering five and a half acres and containing over three hundred animals. The nerve center was the steam power plant, always alive, its fiery maw glowing day and night.

Ben followed the road to the central building, a heavy, log structure, two stories high. He dismounted before a roofed hitching rack and stepped onto the porch. A hallway led him to Cal Runyon's office, identified by gilt lettering on the pine-paneled door:

CALVIN D. RUNYON
GENERAL SUPERINTENDENT
CALIFORNIA-OREGON LUMBER AND
MILLING COMPANY

Ben Colfax knocked and heard Runyon's grumbled invitation to enter. Runyon was at his desk, coatless, sleeve-garters holding the cuffs of his silk shirt free of the litter of papers. A fire glowed in the corner stove, crowding a stuffy heat into the room. Runyon looked up when Colfax stepped in, then said, "Surprised to see you, Ben. There's whiskey and cigars on the sideboard."

Colfax flung open a window, admitting a shot of cold air and the pungent flavors of a saturated forest. "What are you trying to do, kiln-dry yourself?" He made an adjustment of the stove, then helped himself to the whiskey and cigars. "Shouldn't do this," he said with a sigh. "Bothers my indigestion so late at night." He eased himself into a chair, shot glass in one hand, cigar between his teeth. "How's Pete's head? The Kid fetched him a couple of good ones."

"I had to cool him down. He wanted to take his gun and shoot it out with the Kid,"

Cal Runyon admitted. He pushed his work aside and folded his hands. "Ben, just what did the old man get us into with this Wind River Kid?"

"Trouble more than likely," Colfax said. He puffed on his cigar and tried valiantly to come up with a smoke ring. Finally he gave it up. "What the hell got into the old man, Cal? He spooked?"

"Mad at you and Bess," Runyon said. "Ben, he didn't shoot her father. And when she accused him of it, he swore he'd slap her down hard."

Ben Colfax pawed at his mustache. "Cadmus did some rantin' and ravin', somethin' about kickin' me out of office, this being election time. But I really didn't take him serious, Cal."

"Neither did I," Runyon admitted. "This rocked me, Ben, because I've been relying on you to keep the peace. Cadmus is an old fire-eater, Ben; you know that. Sometimes I think he'll just up and take a rifle and settle his differences. He worries me."

"You ain't the only one," Colfax said. "Couldn't you have stopped him from pulling this fool election stunt?"

"I tried to talk to him, but he wouldn't listen." Runyon chuckled. "He knew I'd be against it, so he kept it from me until it was too late to do anything about it. When he gets his wind up, there's no stopping him." He leaned forward, his manner suddenly serious. "But this Wind River Kid scares me. He doesn't push worth a damn and the old man's liable to get shot for his trouble. We've got to do something about it, Ben."

"Do? Hell, do what?"

"Get the Kid out of town, or get Bess Jamison to cool down for awhile."

"Can't see her doing that," Ben Colfax confessed. "Bess has some real hard feelings toward Cadmus. You blame her?"

"No, no," Cal Runyon said. He got up and closed the window, then stood there watching the rain smear the glass. "Ben, I'm going, to be on the square with you. I can do it now because you're on the outside." He turned about to face Ben Colfax. "If anything ever pushed Cadmus Rindo into the fight, he'd fold and this town would fold with him. Rindo gave away a lot, but he took a lot back." Runyon opened a filing cabinet and tossed a thick sheaf of papers on the desk. "These are notes, Ben. All signed by Cadmus Rindo. There aren't a dozen men in this town who don't hold Rindo's note." He waved his hands to include the mill and all the buildings. "Where do you think the money came from to build all this, Ben?

Small investors, that's where. Ben, if the old man ever showed the least sign of being shaky, the people who hold his notes would sell out at twenty-five cents on the dollar. If that happened, Rindo's Springs would be dead."

Ben Colfax clung to a thoughtful silence, his eyes veiled and secretive. "Can't he pay 'em off, Cal?"

"In ten years, or five if he was pressed. Ben, the country needs timber. We've grown so fast we haven't caught up yet. Nothing's laid by for that rainy day."

"Rainin' now," Colfax said softly.

Cal Runyon understood what he meant and his face settled into troubled lines. "Ben, I think I know you. You've lived a lifetime being honest and fair to everyone. Will you try and convince Bess that she'll only destroy herself if she tries to stir up trouble now?"

"I'll do what I can," Colfax promised and stood up. Cal Runyon started around his desk but Colfax waved him back. "Know my own way out, Cal. Thanks for the cigar and drink, although I'll likely toss all night."

Walking slowly down the hall, Ben Colfax gnawed the cigar. On the porch he paused to contemplate the rain and the dreary night. His lips drew into a thoughtful pucker; his eyebrows twisted into crooked thickets. "That close, eh?" he said very softly. "Well I'll be doggoned!"

Then he stepped out into the downpour and swung into a soggy saddle.

4

Since that agony-filled day eight years before when Will Beau-Haven slipped and found his hips hopelessly crushed beneath a legging arch's iron-bound wheel, he had been making it his habit to sit on the upper gallery of his hotel and observe the town of Rindo's Springs. A man with considerable time on his hands soon learns to spend it carefully, and Will Beau-Haven had always considered himself a thrifty man.

Promptly at eight each morning his wife, Grace, pushed him onto the porch in a special, wheeled chair, placed a robe over his withered legs, then left him to watch the town. By his side was a tin pail on which a long cord was attached, and at nine-thirty Will Beau-Haven hailed a ragged-haired boy, lowered the bucket, then watched the lad trot across the street to Burkhauser's saloon. A moment later the boy returned, the bucket now full of beer. The rope was retied and the bucket hoisted aloft; a coin was dropped to the boy's eager hand.

In this quiet way Will Beau-Haven spent his days, and shortly after one o'clock, when *The Rindo County Free Press* reached the streets, Beau-Haven again lowered his line to receive his paper. Not that it would contain anything he didn't already know, but he was a man who enjoyed having his observations substantiated by the printed word.

Unfolding the paper, Will Beau-Haven read the banner line, then let his eyes jump to the center column that ran the length of the page, printed in type so bold as to prohibit anyone missing it. He read the account twice, then called his wife to the porch. She was a woman in her early thirties, quite pretty in a quiet way. Her dress was brown and severely devoid of trim. She wore her hair simply parted, then coiled into an unimaginative bun on the back of her head. Seemingly she took pains to make herself as unattractive as possible; still, a native beauty refused to be hidden — she could not disguise the appealing bow of her lips, the deep color of her eyes, or the exciting swell of breast and hip.

While she stood there, Will Beau-Haven read aloud the enumerated deeds of the

Wind River Kid, and at the completion of this third reading, he still could not decide whether the Kid was saint or sinner. By clinging to the proven record, Nan Buckley had written with startling objectivity, presenting a man no different from most, save that all his dirty linen had been hauled out at one time and aired publicly.

"I think it's a disgrace," Grace Beau-Haven said flatly, "having a man like that in public office. Why, it says right there he's wanted in Arizona."

Then, like most men presented with a flat statement, Will Beau-Haven began to argue with his wife, taking the Kid's side. Standing half-hidden in her own doorway, Nan Buckley observed this, and the duplication of it up and down the main street, wherever men gathered.

Gabe, her typesetter, eased up and said, "Started something, Nan." He waved his hand at the street. "They'll argue this for a month."

"You have to believe in something to argue," she said softly.

The old man looked at her, then his face wrinkled into a grin. "I see it now. Smart. Very smart. The Kid didn't have a friend in town, so you organized them for him."

"Why not?" she asked. "Gabe, I've never

seen people agree on everything. But a man has to declare himself before others will take a side, for or against." She reached behind her and picked up a paper. "The Wind River Kid has declared himself. Look at this last paragraph:

'This is the duly elected peace officer of Rindo County, a man no different from other men, no more misunderstood, no more maligned. How are we to judge this man? By the record, or by his conduct in Rindo's Springs? Like all of us, the Wind River Kid must endure the day-by-day judgments of his fellow men. Are you, as a citizen of Rindo's Springs, prepared to judge?' "

"Well," Gabe admitted, "if it was calculated to start argument, you sure done what you set out to do."

"I think I'll take a walk through town," Nan said. A glance at the curdled sky told her that the rain had passed, so she took a shawl instead of a parasol. The street was a mire of mud and a heavy-laden lumber wagon drove through, the wheels gouging deep grooves in the earth. Nan walked slowly along the main street, her ears picking up bits of argument as she passed chattering groups. At a side street she turned, walking along until the street dwindled to a buggy lane, at whose end sat the most imposing home in Rindo's Springs. It had been a year in the building; most of the gable work and gingerbread was hand-carved and shipped overland from San Francisco after a stormy passage through the Roarin' Forties. The house was surrounded by an acre of lawn, and a bronze deer browsed under the stately trees.

Lifting a large metal knocker in the center of the door, Nan rapped a few times and heard the echo boom through the house. A moment later a colored servant came to the door.

"I'd like to speak to Mr. Rindo, please," Nan said.

"He's in the drawin' room, Ma'am."

She knew the way, and when she stepped into the large room, she closed the door. Pale pine panels ran to the ceiling; beneath her feet was a thick, maroon rug. A chandelier, reported to have cost several thousand dollars, hung on a brass chain from the beamed ceiling. The air was saturated with the odor of Rindo's cigars and wood smoke, the residue of a badly drawing fireplace. Cadmus Rindo sat in his deep chair facing a broad window which fronted on the lane leading in. He spoke without turning his head. "Saw you come in." He gestured to the paper flung haphazardly on the floor. "Read that too. What are you trying to start?"

Nan came around and sat down so that she could see his face. "I just wanted the citizens to know what kind of a man you elected."

He looked at her quickly, his eyes tight-pinched and knife-sharp. "So you think he's my man, is that it?"

"You put him in office."

He shook his head, a loose lock of hair bobbing. His flesh was dark and dryly wrinkled, like old leather, yet his eyes were as clear as a still pond, and his hands were without tremor. "I picked a dark horse as a means of getting to Ben," he said. "But that same horse turned right around and kicked me when I tried to mount him."

"That was your mistake," Nan said flatly. "Dealing off the bottom is an expert's business; it's not your game."

He glared at her. "You going to lecture me?" His anger was a sham and they both knew it. Suddenly he smiled and pawed his mouth out of shape. "Nan, you're always tryin' to beard the lion in his own den."

"I like you," she said simply. "Even when

you're as fretful as a back-sore mule." She fell silent momentarily, then added, "You've never liked Ben Colfax, have you?"

"No, I haven't," Rindo admitted. "I've always distrusted a man who was apparently so blamed good all the time." He moved his hands restlessly. "Damn it, Nan, I only wanted him out of office, and for no other reason than I just don't trust him. Didn't give a damn who I elected in his place either. When I saw the Wind River Kid gettin' drunk in Burkhauser's place, I got the idea of running him against Ben. Be a big insult to Ben." He blew out a long breath. "Of course the Jamison girl's convinced that it's all an attempt to buy the law for my side."

"What else could she think?" Nan asked. "Mr. Rindo, you sicked Pete Davis into breaking that window to prove you had the law bought and paid for. Only the Kid fooled you, didn't he?"

"Yeah, he did! I got a right to test a man, haven't I?" He chuckled. "I sure found out in a hurry too." He looked steadily at Nan Buckley. "But I did it for my own pure pleasure." He waved his hands. "The Jamison girl believes that I want to own the law. Ben Colfax has always believed that. Consarn it, Nan, it's just that I don't trust the man!"

Nan Buckley stood up. "I have things to do. Perhaps I'll stop by later."

"Do that," Cadmus Rindo said. He pulled a bell cord near his chair and a moment later the servant appeared. "Show Miss Buckley out, Jules."

Walking slowly down the path, Nan considered Rindo's conversation. Colfax was not the only man in Rindo's Springs the old man didn't cotten to; Burkhauser was high on the list. In times past, Cadmus Rindo had never imposed his will on anyone. Nan found it difficult to believe that he had changed his policy. Even George Jamison, Bess's father, had failed to rile the old man past the argument stage.

Nan stopped at the sheriff's office and found it empty. When she saw the badge on the desk, she drew her conclusion and hurried back to the newspaper office. She found a small boy playing on the boardwalk, and after giving him a dime, dispatched him to the stable with orders to have her buggy hitched.

Going to her room, she shut the door and quickly shed dress and petticoats. She slipped into a pair of faded man's jeans and a shirt, then rolled a heavy coat inside her slicker.

From the cupboard she took cold meat, a

loaf of bread, and two cans of peaches. Placing these in a flour sack, she added a can opener, knife and spoon. On her way to the stable, she stopped again at the sheriff's office only long enough to pick up the tarnished badge. Her buggy was waiting and as she mounted, the hostler said, "Cloudin' up, Miss Buckley."

"The roof doesn't leak," she said and whipped out of town, taking the west road. A man on the move, she decided, would not retrace his steps, and the Wind River Kid had drifted in from the east. He'd go west, probably to Pendleton, then turn south, toward California.

For better than an hour she drove at a steady pace, and later, when she came to the road leading to Bess Jamison's place, she turned off. The rain was still running off from the highland, and in some places it roared and ripped alongside the road, turning the ditches into unruly torrents.

Rain has always been the nemesis of logging, and Bess' crew was working close to camp, making repairs on wagons and logging arches, getting ready for the drying wind and time when falling would commence.

As Nan wheeled up to the porch and dismounted, Bess came to the doorway, nodded indifferently. No great friendship existed between them, yet there had never been an open animosity either. Bess held the door open so Nan could step into the house. She wiped her feet on some burlap sacks.

"You don't get out this way often," Bess Jamison said. Moving into the drab parlor, she motioned Nan into a hard-backed chair. The room was quite plain; her father had had next to nothing when he first came to this country and time hadn't added substantially to his possessions.

"I was wondering," Nan said, "if you had seen the new sheriff?"

"Only that once in jail," Bess admitted. She bit her lip. "I'm afraid I gave him a rather poor impression. But I was angry. That's why I let Harry try to — well, teach him a thing or two."

"But I understand Harry got the lesson," Nan said. She folded her hands. "That hardly seems important now, Bess. I just talked to Cadmus Rindo and I don't think he tried to buy the law just to get at you."

"He's lying," Bess said flatly. She wiped a hand across her face, then brushed stray strands of hair from her forehead. "I accused him of killing my father, and Cadmus Rindo has never taken a thing like that from anyone. Why does he keep a gunman on the payroll if it isn't to threaten me?"

"Believe me, Bess, he only intended to hurt Ben."

She blew a gusty breath of disbelief through her nose. "Now that's downright ridiculous. Ben's a good man; everyone likes him." She looked steadily at Nan Buckley. "I suppose you talked to Cal Runyon too."

This was supposed to hurt, and it must have found a mark for Nan's chin lifted slightly and her eyes turned brightly brittle. "Cal and I haven't spoken for six months," she said. "I hope you believe that because it's true."

"You're still in love with him," Bess accused.

"Of course," Nan said softly. "But Cal made his choice; I've stepped aside. What are you going to do about him, Bess?"

"That's my business," she said cooly.

"Not exactly. I stepped aside for you, Bess, but I didn't do it so you could throw him over any time you felt like it." She stood up and moved to the door. "Please understand me. You either make up your mind about Cal Runyon, or I'll move in on your territory."

"If he'll take you it'll be second best as far

as he's concerned," Bess stated. "He loves me."

"Then you're a bigger fool than I thought," Nan said and went to her buggy. She did not bother with a goodbye. Wheeling out of the yard, she drove the treacherous logging trail to the main road, then turned west again.

The sky was muddy and dreary, and a short time later rain began to fall again. She put her poncho around her legs and listened to the rain rattle on the buggy top. Talking about Cal Runyon had left her with an empty feeling, one she had thought herself rid of months ago.

The road wound through heavily timbered land, and at times clung to the sloped sides of mountains that were veiled at the tops. Once she had to pull to the side of the road to let the Dallas Stage wheel by, high wheels flinging mud, side curtains flapping. The passengers waved and shouted greetings, then passed from her view, leaving her only the drum of the rain for company.

By late afternoon she sighted the half-abandoned town of Sinking Wells. Started ten years before by three Eastern promoters, Sinking Wells was going to be the hub of a vast railroad system linking Oregon with points east, or so the promoters claimed. Within five months, Sinking Wells boasted ten thousand citizens, but the railroad died in the dream stage, and since the citizens had come seeking quick money, they had moved on, leaving four through streets and a score of rotting buildings. Recalling the unsuccessful attempts made to revitalize Sinking Wells, Nan Buckley was convinced that once a town died, it could never be brought back. Her one concern was that Rindo's Springs would suffer a similar fate, and she meant to prevent that if she could.

Driving past the sagging hotel, Nan Buckley pulled in near the one section of hitching rack still standing. The only place of business was the hotel, and this was slowly going to pieces. The porch sagged dangerously and dribbled water through the roof in several spots. Stepping inside, Nan saw that part of the old saloon's bar had been set up in the lobby, and along one wall, bins from the mercantile had been set up to make Sinking Wells a one-man operation.

The owner and sole citizen was an ancient man whose only title to all this was the fact that he had remained behind while the others had left. He looked around when Nan came in, stomping mud from her boots.

"You want a room?" he asked.

She shook her head.

"A drink then?"

Again she shook her head.

The old man mauled his whiskers. "Can't make a nickel that way." He snapped his fingers. "You're looking for somebody? A man, twenty-five or so, brown eyes and hair, and wearin' a canvas brush jacket." His eyes pulled into fleshy slits. "Upstairs. He bought a bottle and that's the last I've seen of him."

"Thanks," Nan said and went up the creaky steps. On the upper landing she paused, looking at the double row of closed doors. Then she walked along, bending down to study each knob. When she found one with disturbed dust, she knocked. For a moment she thought that she had made a poor guess, then the Kid said, "Hell, it's open if you want in."

Taking a deep breath, Nan opened the door and stepped inside. The Kid was stretched out on the rickety bed. Water dribbled down one wall, making a puddle on the floor. Then he swung his feet to the floor and sat up.

"Hello," Nan said.

"What do you want, Miss Buckley?"

"You didn't stay to read my story," she said.

"I already know the story," he said.

Nan walked deeper into the room, picked up the bottle of whiskey she saw sitting on the dilapidated dresser and saw that it had never been uncorked. She put it back.

"Why haven't you opened it?"

"I could have been waiting for company," he said. He sagged back on the bed and placed his hands behind his head. "Why don't you go back to Rindo's Springs where you belong?"

There were no chairs in the room so the Kid moved his feet aside, making a place on the edge of the bed where she could sit. He watched her with unwavering attention, then said, "If people knew you followed me here, they might draw some wrong conclusions."

"That doesn't worry me," Nan said. "Where are you going from here? California?"

"I hear it's nice there. Lots of sunshine."

"Perhaps it's best that you do go," she said softly. "You've gotten into the habit of running and you've tried to drink yourself into forgetfulness. The next thing will be to change your name, won't it?"

This angered him. "Why the hell would I do that?"

"Another form of denial," she said. "If the running can't make you forget who you are, and the whiskey can't, then changing your name might."

"Thanks for the lecture," the Kid said. "If you're through, will you get out so I can enjoy my bottle?"

"Oh, I intend to," Nan said easily. "But I don't think you'll enjoy it any more than you enjoyed it in Rindo's Springs." She clasped her hands together and smiled faintly. "You see, I believe in the Wind River Kid. That may sound strange, having known you for such a short time, but it's still true. Like it or not, you were elected sheriff of Rindo County. Please come back. We need you."

He sat up, facing her. "I can make you leave," he said. "Do you want me to?"

"I'm not leaving yet," she said. "And I think I know —"

He cut her off when he put his arms around her and pressed his lips on hers. There was gentleness in him, but he put it aside for a purposeful roughness, and she submitted to his embrace not stiffly but with a relaxed deadness. Slowly he released her and stood up, his back to her.

"Now I feel ashamed of myself," he said. "You want to hate me, go ahead."

"I can understand you," Nan said. "Much better than you think I do." She stood up and touched him lightly on the arm. "Sooner or later every man on this earth has to declare himself as standing for something. You think that what people think about you can hurt you? No, it really can't. But what you think about yourself can hurt you."

Perhaps because he stood so unmoving she felt that what she said fell on deaf ears; her manner suddenly changed and she became very much in a hurry. Moving to the door, she said, "Well, I've had my say. Goodbye."

He did not move until she started down the hall, then he bolted after her. "Nan!" Slowly she turned around and looked at him. "Nan, I've got a tired horse. Can you give me a lift back?"

Her smile seemed to brighten the drab hall. She came up to him and took his arm. "Of course. Let's go."

"Wait," he said and went back inside the room. When he came out he was carrying the whiskey bottle. Downstairs he paused long enough to give it back to the old man. "Just hand it to the next dry man who comes through."

"What happens if I get dry myself?" the old man asked.

The Kid grinned. "Don't you know what to do?"

They stepped out into the smothering rain. The Kid got his horse and tied it behind the buggy, then handed Nan up to the seat. He drove into the first gloom of night while Nan tucked the poncho around their legs.

For awhile they rode along without talk, then the Kid said, "You said you understood how it was with me because of your father. You want to tell me?"

"I guess," she said. "He was a newspaper man in San Francisco, but he made a serious mistake: he backed the wrong political candidate. There was an investigation, and a scandal, and when the smoke cleared, Dad was as black as the blackest. So he packed everything that was left and we started moving. Running is the word. As soon as he would be recognized, he'd move again. Until we came to Rindo's Springs. There he stayed and faced the world."

"How was it?" he asked softly.

"Not easy, but he lived like he wanted to live, and he ran an honest newspaper. Last year he died of consumption."

"Too bad," he murmured. "But a lot of him rubbed off on you, Nan."

"I like to think that it did," she said. "Rindo's Springs needed my father, and he needed Rindo's Springs."

"And you think I'm like that?"

She smiled. "I know you are."

A distant streak of lightning cut a ragged path to the earth and thunder boomed. Rain rattled on the tight buggy top and the horses hoofs threw mud against the bangboard. The Kid looked at her a moment, then said, "Nan, I'd like you to know something. I'm not sorry I kissed you."

"I know," she said.

"And you?"

She smiled and shook her head. "Don't pin me down."

He was wise enough to know that he could go no farther, so he changed the subject. "Nan, do you think I can be a good sheriff?"

"You know the answer to that," she said. "I talked to Cadmus Rindo and he respects you."

This struck him as funny. "He ordered me out of town!"

"That should convince you that I'm right," Nan said. "But knowing Cadmus as I do, I'd say that he'll have Pete try to get rid of you." She took his arm and held it until he looked at her. "I want you to know that I'm for the old man. I believe he has a right to what's his. If anything happened to Cadmus Rindo, the town would die. And dead towns never come back, Kid. Name me one that has."

He paused for a moment, his brows furrowed. "I guess I can't."

"You see? Cadmus Rindo gave nearly everyone there a start, and many of them were men already convinced that they would never get a second chance. In return, they've invested in Rindo's lumber mill. He alone holds everything together. That's why nothing must happen to him, Kid. That's why Rindo's Springs needs you."

"You want a miracle?" he asked.

"If it takes one, yes. Kid, will you talk with the old man?"

"Before or after he runs me out of town?"

This was a question she didn't know how to answer, and he didn't press her for one. They settled back, letting the soggy miles disappear beneath the iron-shod wheels.

5

Nan Buckley stopped at the jail; the Kid had said he preferred the solitary cot to a room at the hotel. Then she drove down the street to the newspaper office while the Kid watched. When he entered the office it was dark and he stumbled about, trying to find the lamp. With it lit, he went into the small room and tugged off his boots. Settling back, he thought about Nan Buckley and that brief interval of time when he had held her in his arms.

The thought contained an element of excitement for him; no other woman had given him that feeling. And he had known a few women, and now that he put his mind to it, could recall several with varying degrees of clarity. There was that Mexican girl in Laredo; he could not remember her name, but he remembered Laredo and Joel McKitrich; the town had been theirs while the job lasted. But a gun job never did last long. In Tucson there had been Helen; he supposed he could have married her if her father hadn't been a judge. What he remembered best about Cheyenne was Jane, but a man can't fight nesters with one hand and marry into them with the other.

A knock at the outer door broke off his reverie and he padded to the front of the building in his stocking feet. He opened the door and was surprised to find Cadmus Rindo standing there, slicker spilling water.

"Kind of late, I know," Rindo said, "but one of my boys saw you come back to town."

"Come on in," the Kid said, closing the door. Rindo shrugged out of his raincoat and took off his hat. He laid these on the desk, then said, "If Nan had minded her own business, you'd be a long way from here by now, and the only one who would have been disappointed is Pete Davis."

"More than likely," the Kid admitted. "That shouldn't make you cry."

"Now, no need to get a chip on your shoulder," Rindo said. "I've been doing some serious thinking since we last met." He glanced briefly at the young man. "Seems that I'll have to get along with you, Kid. At least it'll be better than fighting Ben Colfax."

"Just what's wrong with Ben?" the Kid asked. "Besides sticky fingers when it comes to money."

"Ha!" Rindo shouted, slapping the desk. "So you see it too. Good. Makes things easier for me." He perched on the corner of the desk. "I'll come right to the point. What started out of spite toward Ben Colfax has turned into something else now. I never trusted Ben because he always acted too damn good. No man's really that way. Got to be something wrong or he ain't human." He squinted his eyes. "Expect you're trying to make sense of what I'm saying. Well, it's simple enough. I don't want trouble with you, Kid."

"If you're offering to buy —"

"Oh, for Christ's sake!" Rindo exploded, looking disgusted. "Kid, you think I got horns or something?" He chuckled. "Nan reminded me that I threatened you. Well, I was mad. Any man would be mad when his plans kick back at him." He rubbed his gnarled hands together, groping for words. "I got a sick town here, Kid. Too many people wanting what don't belong to 'em in the first place. I know, I'm an old hog who saw this first and wanted it for himself. That was a young man's natural greed, but I'm not young anymore. Be eighty next month, which is more time than a man's generally allowed on this earth. Gettin' tired too. For some years now I've been wantin' to give away what I worked so hard to get, but it's a hard task to feed a hungry dog when he keeps snappin' at your hand."

"This Jamison woman — you'd give her the land she wants?"

Cadmus Rindo paused with the packing of his pipe and nodded.

The Wind River Kid said, "If you do, she'll take it for a sign of weakness. That'll spread and every merchant in town will feel shaky because they have their money tied up in your outfit."

Rindo scratched a match across his boot sole. "You see it," he said. "No need to explain it to you. Hell of a mess when a man can't get rid of what he has."

"The Jamison woman thinks you killed her father," the Kid said.

"I didn't shoot him," Rindo said flatly. "Hell, I wanted to bad enough at times, but when I kill a man it's in broad daylight where people can see it." His pipe gurgled when he drew on it and he paused to clean out the stem with a straw he kept pocketed for that purpose. "Takes money to set up a big mill, Kid." He tapped himself on the chest. "I have the mill, so Bess Jamison hauls the logs to me for milling. The trouble comes when the sawed stuff is loaded on her wagons. She scales the logs, and then scales the lumber when it's loaded, then claims that I'm shorting her. Hell, if Pete wasn't around to scare 'em a little I'd have had serious trouble before this."

"Tell her to mill the stuff somewhere else," the Kid suggested.

The old man snorted. "Can't do that, son. Hell, she'd be shooting at me inside of a week. Besides, I'm not after her." He shook his head. "Can't convince her or Ben Colfax of that though. The way they tell it, I just go around crackin' the whip. Anyway, old man Jamison kept accusing me of cheating him by holding back some of his sawed lumber out of every load. I just took it at first, then when he kept it up, I sent Cal Runyon with a message, saying that I wanted to have a talk and settle the squabble. The whole damn town knew there was bad blood between us, so when Jamison got shot on the company steps, I was the prime suspect."

"But you didn't shoot him, you say."

"Hell no, I didn't! Heard the shot, grabbed my own pistol and ran out. A crowd started to gather and then Ben Colfax came up. He grabbed the gun out of my hand and held me for the coroner's inquest. They turned me loose." He studied the grain in his pipe for a moment. "Still, there's a lot of folks who think I did it."

"Ben Colfax one of them?"

"Yep," Rindo said. "That's why I wanted Ben out of office. He was only interested in gettin' me, not helping the town."

"Well, you sure didn't help it by shoving me down the voters' throats," the Kid said. "Mr. Rindo, you've got to stop doing what's right for people. Let them do for themselves."

"Hell, they'll go under!"

"That's every man's privilege," the Kid said. "You elected me sheriff and I'll keep the peace if I can. But if you pull another stunt like sicking your gunman on me, I'll throw you in jail along with him."

Cadmus Rindo stared at him. "You mean that," he said.

"Try me and see," the Kid invited. "I know Pete feels he's got to even the score, but tell him not to try it with a gun."

Rindo grunted and got up, putting on his slicker and hat. "We'll get along, you and me." He stepped out into the slanting rain and got into his waiting buggy. The Kid stood in the doorway as the old man drove down the dark street. When Rindo turned the far corner, the Kid moved to close the door, then paused when he saw a man leave the shadows across the street. The man hurried across the street and only when he reached the near boardwalk did the Kid recognize Ben Colfax.

"Been makin' a deal?" Colfax asked. Water ran in streaks down his face and his heavy coat was soaked through. He hunched his shoulders, trying to ward off the chill night wind.

"Don't say too much," the Kid suggested. "It's late, Ben."

"Late?" Colfax laughed. "Rindo's bought himself a real tough boy this time, ain't he? Well, I'm pretty good myself; age ain't slowed me down. Just remember that when you get set to crowd me."

"No one's crowding you," the Kid said. He began to close the door, but Ben Colfax flung out his arm.

"Hold on! I'm not through talkin'."

"Tell me about it in the morning," the Kid said and shoved hard on the door. Ben thrust his shoulder forward, again blocking it, only this time, the Kid suddenly released the door, allowing Colfax to plunge into the room.

The ex-sheriff would have sprawled on his face had not the Kid's fist whistled up and smashed him in the mouth. Colfax reeled backward, catching his bootheel on the boardwalk edge. Arms flailing, Ben Colfax landed flat in the muddy street. The Kid flung the door wide and looked at the man, waiting patiently while Colfax sat up, pawing at the mud that clung to him.

"Believe me now?" the Kid asked. He shut the door then and slid the bolt. An instant later, Ben Colfax hammered on the panel, then gave up and went away. The Wind River Kid returned to his cot and stretched out again, this time snuffing out the lamp.

He listened for a time to the rain drumming on the roof, then sleep tuned the sound out of his consciousness. How long he slept was a question in his mind when a heavy pounding on the door brought him bolt upright. Without lighting the lamps or picking up his gun, he went to the front office, still half asleep.

When the Kid tried to slide the ash bolt, he found it jammed and for a moment could not understand this. Then he realized that someone was putting so much pressure on the outside that it was wedging the wood tight. "All right! All right!" he said. "Get your shoulder off it!"

The weight slacked off and he slid the bar back. Before he could back away, the door crashed in, and the shadowed jumble of three men tried to crowd through at the same time. Had they not been in such a hurry, they would have succeeded in taking him then and there, but he gained a second's grace, and struck before they did. His knuckles caught one man on the bridge of the nose, making him bleat out in pain.

Then all three of the men were in the room; one tried to tackle the Kid around the waist but before the groping arms could restrict him completely, he laced his fingers together and brought both arms down across the back of the man's neck. With a sigh, the man wilted, but the Kid got his feet tangled and fell.

The third man jumped him and in the darkness nearly landed astraddle, but the Kid rolled, taking the man's knees full on the thigh. He sucked in his breath, fearing that his leg was broken; at first it went numb, then started to throb so badly that he was weak with pain. The man who had taken the punch in the nose was up again and swinging his boots. One lucky kick caught the Kid on the shoulder and flung him against the wall. In the darkness identification was impossible; the booted man kicked the wrong man and drew a snarled curse from his partner. They began to grope for the Kid; the downed man stirred and sat up, then got to his feet. He started to say something, then stopped as though he feared the sound of his voice might lead to an identification later.

The Kid held himself absolutely still, blending with the shadows along the base of the wall. His thigh and shoulder sent constant shooting pains through his body, making him strangely light-headed. One of the men stepped close to him and the Kid suddenly reached out and grabbed both ankles, jerking the man backwards, flat on the plank floor. The breath left him in a rush, and the Kid yelled, "I got him!"

Immediately the other two jumped their partner, lacing him with kicks and savage blows. He began to yell and the Kid eased along the wall, moving toward his back room and the .44 hanging there. The man's yelling finally got through to his partners and they stopped pummeling him, realizing that they had the wrong man.

Suddenly, springing to his feet, the Kid made his room in one-legged hops. In a group they started after him, but Pete Davis' voice yelled, "He's after his gun!"

They all made the front door together and fought to get through. The Kid had his .44 now and was swinging around with it.

Leveling it, he fanned it empty, realizing as he shot that he was seconds tardy. Several of his bullets brought down glass across the street, and when the booming echoes died, he could hear the fading pound of boots on the boardwalk.

Tossing his gun on the cot, he limped painfully over to the chest of drawers and put a match to the lamp. Then he sat down on his bed and patiently tried to massage life back into his leg. He was sure no bones were broken, but he had suffered a terrible bruise. Only by a distinct effort of will did he bring himself to stand on it. He walked into the outer office and looked around for anything that might have been dropped in the scuffle. Spots of blood dotted the floor, attesting to the effectiveness of the first blow struck; but he found nothing else, not even a torn-off button.

The rapid burst of gunfire had jarred a few citizens out of a sound sleep; lights were coming on, while across the street, the merchant whose window had been shattered came down in his nightshirt to make a cursing examination. The Kid lit the two lamps in the office, then limped to the door for a look up and down the rain-pestered street. Other than the curious, there was no one resembling Pete and his two tough friends.

He had a choice, he decided. Either Rindo had lied to him and sent Pete around, or this was Davis' own idea, brought about by his impatience to get even. The last possibility seemed a little far-fetched for he was by nature a patient man; his type of retaliation was more apt to be with a gun and in full view of the public. Which left Cadmus Rindo as the main suspect, but the Kid remembered the old man too clearly, the way he looked, and the tone of his voice; it was hard to imagine him lying.

Quite suddenly Ben Colfax came around the far corner, running toward the jail. He hauled up a dozen yards from the door. The Kid said, "You got here mighty quick, Ben. How did you know where to come?"

"I —" Colfax hesitated, then said, "Bein' a peace officer as long as I have sort of gives me a nose for trouble."

"You could get that nose flattened for sticking it in where it doesn't belong," the Kid said. He stood back from the doorway. "Come in."

While Colfax stomped the mud from his boots, the Kid limped into the back room and came back with his gun and holster. Punching out the spent brass, he reloaded the .44, then slipped it into the leather.

Colfax watched the way he favored his leg.

"You get hurt a little?"

"Not so bad I couldn't leave a mark or two of my own," he said. His glance touched Colfax' face and the puffed lips. The ex-sheriff was squinting at the Kid, his eyes pinched nearly shut. Softly the Kid asked, "Those your boys, Ben? You teaming up with Pete maybe?"

Colfax was the soul of indignation. "Damn you, Kid —" He puffed out his cheeks and spoke more calmly. "I got nothing against you." He raised his hand to his bloated mouth. "This here I can settle myself."

"Make sure you do it to my face," the Kid warned. He raised his head when quick, light steps sounded on the walk. Then Nan Buckley appeared, a slicker wrapped around her. She was without a hat and the rain made a soggy ruin of her hair.

"What — ?"

"Join the party," the Kid invited. His glance touched Colfax briefly. "I don't want to keep you, Ben, so if there's anything on your mind, better say it."

"Came here the first time to offer my help," he said fretfully. "Got a punch in the mouth for my trouble."

"Do I look like I need help?" the Kid asked.

"Every man needs it," Colfax said. "I

know this town. I could be a big help to you."

"Would you really, Ben?"

The older man looked squarely at the Kid. "You don't trust me, I can see that. Don't blame you much. Be suspicious myself was I in your place. But it'd be a shame if you let that pious old buzzard talk you into anything. To hear him tell it, he prays every night."

"Could be he does," the Kid said. He glanced at Nan Buckley and found a sparkle of amusement in her eyes. When Ben Colfax looked around at her, she erased it quickly and presented only a bland inscrutable expression.

Ben Colfax was trying another angle. "I'd make you a good deputy, Kid. Been in harness a good many years and I know a few short cuts."

"The next thing you'll be telling me you're honest," the Kid said.

"Ah," Colfax said, "you're still sore about the money that was under your shirt." He pawed at his mouth. "I'll give it back, Kid. Hell, if it makes that much difference, I'll —"

"You keep it," the Kid said. "Consider it a loan, Ben. When I want it back, I'll just up and take it, same as you did."

The soft threat had subtle weight to it and Ben Colfax looked uneasy. "Well," he said, moving toward the door, "I guess I'll say goodnight."

"And better luck next time, Ben," the Kid said.

He was on his way out when he stopped and turned back. "Kid, you don't think I —" Then he saw that talk was useless. "All right, think it then. But proving it is something else, ain't it?"

"If I ever do prove it, Ben, you'll be the first to know."

When Colfax tromped off down the street, the Kid limped to the door and closed it. Nan Buckley said, "I heard the shooting and I was worried."

"How did you know it was me?"

"I don't think there's anyone besides you in Rindo's Springs who can fan a hammer so the shots just run together, unless it's Pete Davis." Her smile was brief, but tinged with concern. "Those shots had a professional touch behind them."

"Yes," he said, "and the more I think of it, the more I believe that those three toughs had Ben Colfax behind them." He eased himself to the corner of the desk and sat down gingerly, favoring his thigh and shoulder. "I was due for a real stomping, Nan. If it hadn't been so blasted dark, I'd have been on the floor yet."

"Can I print this in the paper?"

He shook his head. "Not just yet. You know the merchant across the street? Good. I'll have to pay for his window and whatever goods was damaged by that hail of lead." He snapped his fingers. "A second sooner and I could have nicked one of 'em. But this leg slowed me up."

"Knowing a little about you," Nan said, "I'd suggest that you keep an eye out for bruises. Likely they'll be wearing a few."

He began to chuckle. "They had one of their own bunch on the floor and were flogging the daylights out of him, thinking it was me."

"It could have been you," she said sternly, "and that's not very funny."

He looked steadily at her. "Nan, we haven't known each other very long, but —"

"No," she said. "Kid, don't say any more now and don't ask me anything." She paused, as though considering something of grave importance. "You'll find out anyway, but I'd rather tell you myself. Until a few months ago I was in love with Cal Runyon, Rindo's head man. But he fell in love with Bess Jamison and I stepped out of the picture. It's still too soon for me to be honest, even with myself. And I don't want to hurt you."

"It's all right," he said. "Are you still in love with Runyon?"

"I don't know," she admitted. "If he came to me tomorrow and asked me to marry him, I don't know what I'd say. The not knowing isn't good. But until I'm sure, it'll have to do." She turned toward the door. "It's late. I'd better get home."

After she left, he slid the ash bolt again, reminding himself not to open it when half-asleep or unarmed. The cot felt lumpy but weariness smoothed it. The pain in his leg and shoulder troubled him and sleep came only in fitful snatches. When he awoke, the gray morning light was streaming through the windows. The rain had stopped and only the drip of the eaves remained.

Getting up, he found his leg so sore that walking was a torture. But he hobbled around, enduring the discomfort, and the enforced use seemed to restore some elasticity. Finally he hobbled out and down the street to the restaurant where he ordered breakfast. Afterward he went to the barber shop for a shave and a bath. When he undressed he saw the huge area of discoloration and sent the barber's boy down the street for some liniment.

The town was coming alive; the mill began its clamor, and along the main street, high-sided lumber wagons hauled toward the railhead five miles west. After his bath and liniment rub, the Kid felt a little better. He paid the barber and had just reached the boardwalk when an excited boy rushed up, panting and trying to talk at the same time.

"Trouble — at the — mill," he said and ran back quickly, as though he were afraid he would miss something.

Speed was out of the question as far as the Kid was concerned, but he headed toward the end of the street at a lope. A crowd began to ease along and he saw Ben Colfax come out of a side street to join this exodus.

At the company gate the guard admitted him, and since Colfax had caught up, let him in also. The gate closed against the curious townspeople, and the Kid cut toward the tie mill. Ben Colfax sided him. "Knew this would happen," he said. "Told you it would."

The Kid spotted the crowd of company men and began to batter his way through. All wagon loading had ceased and men climbed atop the bound lumber for a better view of the trouble.

He could hear the fight long before he could see it. Above the shouted encouragements was the crack of bone against bone. When he reached the core of the gathering he paused; only a fool would rush in without surveying the odds. Automatically he assumed that the trouble had started between a Jamison driver and Pete Davis; he could not help but think how neatly this would disguise any bruises picked up last night. Two men circled each other, both bloody and both eager to draw more blood. One was dragging a whip — that would be the teamster, Bess Jamison's man. Pete Davis was armed with a logging peavey and he had used it, for the sharp metal end was crimson.

From the other side of the circle, Cal Runyon was shouting something about being let-through-here-by-God. At that moment the Kid chose to step in between the two men. He faced Pete Davis, luckily, for the man swung the peavey. The Kid ducked and the pole sent his hat spinning into the crowd. Ordinarily he would have closed with the man, but his injured leg prevented that. When Pete back-handed for another swing, the Kid stepped within reach, drew his gun and chopped the man's forearm with the barrel.

The peavey was dropped immediately and the Kid faced Bess Jamison's teamster. "Do I have to take that whip away from you, mister?" His voice was soft, but no one missed the menace in it. The whip dropped almost silently to the mud.

Cal Runyon burst through then, saw the situation was under control and did not interfere. He waved his hand, bringing two men forward. "Get him to the office, then call the doctor."

But the teamster stood his ground, blood dripping from a cut on his head. The Kid said, "Did you start this?"

"Any reason why I should?"

"Don't get smart with me," the Kid advised. "You can talk here or in jail. Make your choice."

"He shorted me again," the teamster said. "Hell, I can tell a full load when I see one. This is shy a hundred feet or better."

"No one has cheated you," Cal Runyon said flatly. "I can show you the papers —"

With a wave of his hand the teamster cut him off. "To hell with your papers!" He glared at Runyon, and then at the Kid. "Figured you'd side with Rindo. He paid for you."

"Take your load and get out of here," the Kid said. "Go on before there's more trouble."

"Sure, but you won't always be able to do this so easy. One of these days we'll all come in and then we'll get a square deal or there'll be dead men."

He whirled and mounted his wagon. Ben Colfax stepped forward and said, "I know this man well. Maybe if I rode along with him I could talk sense to him."

"Why don't you keep your nose out of it?" the Kid asked.

Colfax smiled. "Why, there ain't nothin' about this that's official, sheriff. You got any objections to lettin' me ride with a friend?" He turned and got into the wagon.

The crowd opened a lane so the wagon could pass. The Kid turned and waited while Cal Runyon dispersed the men back to their jobs. Finally Runyon said, "Damn it, I hate these things."

"Both of you can't be right," the Kid said. "You're sure they're getting —"

"Hell yes, I'm sure," Runyon said. His young face was grave with genuine worry, the face of a man who preferred to live simply and in peace, but whose job was neither peaceful nor simple. "You handled Pete a little rough. Was it necessary?"

"You think I should have let him crown me with that peavey?"

Runyon shook his head. "He's a hothead. I'll try and cool him off enough so he won't take a gun to you. Pete's that way. To really lick him you'd have to kill him."

"I wouldn't want to do that, but his pride may force a showdown between us."

"It's hell," Runyon admitted. "That's the trouble with trying to settle a fight where both men think they're right. The one you lean on always feels that he got the short end." He looked at the Kid. "Can you come to my office?"

"Sure," the Kid said and limped along beside Runyon.

After a time, Runyon's curiosity got the best of him. "Did Pete give you that limp?"

"Yeah. Last night around midnight," the Kid said. They entered the main building and Runyon saw that the sheriff had a drink of good whiskey and a fine cigar. Then the young engineer went behind his desk and sat down, cocking his feet up on the edge.

"Ben was trying to help. I suppose you know that," Runyon said.

"No, I didn't know it. He a friend of yours?"

"I like Ben," Runyon admitted. He gnawed on his cigar, his eyes thoughtful. "You know, one of these days Cadmus Rindo's going to get damn tired of this squabble and order a clean-up. Likely I'll be the man appointed for the job."

"Will you do it?"

"Either do it or quit," Runyon said. "But I like my job."

"Even if it included running Bess Jamison off her place?"

Runyon frowned deeply, indicating that he had considered this possibility before. "I suppose you've been told about Bess and me. Fairly common gossip around town." He laughed without humor. "People seem to get a kick out of watching two people tear apart over something they can't help. Like watching a dog fight. I want to marry Bess, but she won't have me unless it's on her terms."

"You mean join her?"

"That's about it," Runyon said.

"What are your terms?"

"The same, only turned around," he admitted. The ease left his expression and a cloud of lines formed on his forehead. "I'll never understand why her father was killed. Before that there was just bad feeling and a lot of talk. Now it's open dislike. Trouble all the time, like today. Every week there's a fight or the threat of one."

"One of these days," the Kid said softly, "a teamster will bring his rifle along. Be sure to call me before Pete Davis makes him use it."

"Have no fear, I will," Runyon said. He paused to study the ash on his cigar a moment. "Did you see what Nan wrote about you in the paper?"

"No," the Kid said.

"Well," Runyon said, unsure of his conversational departure point, "you've been around; let's put it that way." His glance came across the desk very steady. "The fact that you're still here reinforces my first opinion: that you're a man who can draw faster and shoot straighter than most. Of course, there are those who'll treat you like you had the plague. Just something that you'll have to put up with. But while you're letting the cold shoulders bounce off, remember that damn few of us in Rindo's Springs are lily white."

"I've been told that already," the Kid said. "Does that include you?"

"The whole wide world," Runyon said. He walked to the door with the Kid and watched him cross the soggy yard, moving at an easy pace to favor his bruised leg. When the sheriff had passed through the front gate, Runyon locked his office and went to the stable to saddle his horse.

Leaving the grounds by one of the logging

roads, he bypassed the town, then met the main road on the other side. He rode at a steady pace and near noon, cut off toward Bess Jamison's. When he rode into the yard, she came to the porch edge, her hands sheltered by an apron.

Runyon dismounted. "There was trouble again, Bess."

"I'm not surprised," she said. "There'll always be trouble as long as your loader cheats us and Pete stands there to make him take it."

He sighed as a man will when he has made up his mind not to lose his temper. "Can I come in?"

Turning, she went into the house and he followed her into the parlor. She sat down but he remained standing, feeling very ill at ease.

"Bess, every time there's trouble, we just drift farther apart. Is that what you want?"

"We can't always have what we want," she said. "I thought we settled that."

"Settled what? That you'd go your way and I'd go mine? Bess, we love each other. Can you just forget that?"

"I can now," she said. "When my father was alive, everything was different. Now this is my fight. Please don't ask me to forget what he stood for."

He shook his head, blocked by this inflexible argument. "I'm not asking you to forget anything. But we have to bury the past, Bess. What is hating Rindo getting you? You've even forgotten how to smile."

"Don't ask me to change what I am, Cal."

He reached down and took her arm, turning her so that she faced him. "Bess, what do you want of me?" He looked confused, bewildered. "Do you want me to quit Rindo? We can get married and move away somewhere. I can get another job."

"Run?" She seemed outraged. "You'd suggest that I run? When I leave here, if I ever leave, Cadmus Rindo will be on his knees."

This was, he already knew, the point where words failed him completely, and no matter how he tried, he could not sway her. So he quickly pulled her to her feet and against him and pressed his mouth on hers. She slapped him once, then began to push at him, but he held her until her arms went around him. She was a woman of flesh and feeling; he needed no further proof than this. His arms hurt her, a welcome hurt for she moaned and clung to him.

But once free of his embrace, the effect of his love was lost to her. The hard inflexibility returned to her expression and she clenched her fists as tears formed in her eyes. "You have no right to try to make me weak, Cal."

"Bess —"

"Get out," she said softly. "Cal, just get out and leave me alone. Don't come back."

"You don't mean that!"

"I do mean it! I have to mean it!"

He stood there for a moment, hoping she would change her mind, but he understood that she could never change; her hate for Rindo had spread through her until it encompassed many things. So he went outside to his horse, mounted, and rode slowly from the yard. He tried to think of additional arguments, but there were none. The pleasantness had vanished from the day, leaving it dull; the enthusiasm he normally felt toward living drifted to nothing.

She was mistaken, and blind to her error. And it seemed to be Cal Runyon's destiny to stand by, a helpless observer, while Bess Jamison skated along the thin edge of self-destruction.

6

When the Wind River Kid returned to his office, he was not at all surprised to find a delegation of townsmen waiting for him. They stood in a close group, severe of expression, very righteous and hard-minded. The Kid had faced other men like these, men who had little tolerance for anyone outside their own restricted sphere.

He closed the door and said, "This looks official as hell."

A short man in his fifties spoke up. "Allow me to introduce myself. I'm Jake Leggett, the mayor of Rindo's Springs." His round stomach jiggled when he talked and he seemed to be eternally out of breath, for he sucked in whistling draughts of air after every sentence. Leggett did not offer to shake hands and the Kid did not seem offended. "These gentlemen are Dr. Carver, Mr. Osgood, who manages the bank, and Judge Richmond."

Of the four, only Dr. Carver thrust out his hand. He smiled and said, "I'm in your debt, young man. You've already sent me some patients." Carver was a dried-out man, wrinkle-faced, and his clothes bore chemical stains, giving him an untidy appearance. He bent forward suddenly and examined the Kid's eyes. "Ever have any trouble with your liver? No? Good. A healthy liver means a healthy mind. New theory of mine. Haven't got it all worked out yet but it's as promising as some of these new ideas."

Jake Leggett cleared his throat, and Dr. Carver glanced at him, then stepped back. "Mr. — ah — Kid, we consider the election most extraordinary, under the circumstances, and we're at a loss as to what to do about it."

"You waited too long, didn't you? If you had any objections to Cadmus Rindo's electing his own man, you should have protested before this."

"It's not your place to inform us of our duty," Judge Richmond said stiffly. He was a big, florid-faced man who overindulged himself with food and drink, and he obviously loved the sound of his own voice. "Our purpose, sir, is not to discuss what we should or should not have done about the election, but what disposition should be taken with the officer elected." He cleared his throat to get a deeper, more commanding tone. "I feel that it is quite unfortunate that you are not wanted in this state, sir. If that were the case, a warrant for your arrest would solve our problem of removing you from office."

"So that you could put Ben Colfax back in?" the Kid asked.

"Well," Richmond said, "we know Ben to be an honest man."

"He's a petty thief," the Kid said harshly. "And a man who'll steal a small amount will steal more if he gets the chance."

Richmond momentarily puffed his cheeks and sputtered like a freight train trying to make a long grade. "I consider than an insult, sir!" He looked at Carver, Leggett, and Osgood as though expecting them to share his outrage.

"We're not here to argue the virtues of Ben Colfax," Osgood said softly. He was a very small man, barely five foot three, but he had a commanding face and courageous eyes. "Kid, we can't alter the fact that you have a dubious reputation. Not as an outlaw, you understand, but you have been involved in affairs of a violent nature. Naturally, our primary concern is with Rindo's Springs and that it continue to enjoy a healthy atmosphere. We can't tolerate any threat to that atmosphere."

The front door opened suddenly and Nan Buckley stood there. She glanced at each in turn, then came in and shut the door. Jake Leggett said, "This is a private conversation, Miss Buckley."

"There are few private conversations in Rindo's Springs that I don't eventually hear about," Nan said sweetly. "Besides, when I saw this knot of civic virtue gathering, I just had to join it. What would Rindo's Springs do without the guardians of public honesty and morals?"

Judge Richmond was puffing his cheeks in agitation; his frown was a deep weaving of lines across his forehead. "Kid," he said, "I feel it our duty to get up a petition for your removal. That is the only legal recourse available to us."

This was, the Kid knew, what he had always resented and always tried to escape — the brand of the unwanted, this mass condemnation by his contemporaries. Yet, quite strangely, this time he felt no sense of inferiority; he found that he could face them calmly, without a trace of apology or shame. "Now why don't you do that?" he said. "Give you something to do while the Jamison crowd fights it out with Rindo's bunch. Then when the town falls down around your damned ears, you'll know that at least you did your civic duty."

"I can see," Richmond said, "that you force our hand."

"When you use tactics like that," Nan Buckley said, "you force other people to do the same."

Richmond's face grew stern. "I'll not stand for interference now."

This was clearly a warning that Nan Buckley chose to ignore. "Now, Judge, Rindo's Springs is my town too. Or have you spent so much time in Miles City that you've forgotten? Why, just the other day your wife mentioned how much you go to Miles City. She was wondering what the attraction was. I promised to inquire the next time I went there."

"Ah — yes," Richmond said, his face taking on a deeper hue. His glance touched the others. "Gentlemen, if you'll excuse me, I have important matters to attend to."

"What the devil's more important than this?" Mr. Osgood asked impatiently. "Damn it, Freeman, this was your idea in the first place."

"I'm sure it's being left in able hands," Richmond said hastily and stepped outside.

"Fine howdy-do!" Dr. Carver said. "Well, we three are capable, sensible men. There's no reason we can't get on —"

"Doctor," Nan said innocently, "I was talking to Mrs. Fisher, the schoolteacher, the other day. Do you still check her physical condition regularly? We wouldn't want the children of Rindo's Springs to contract a disease, now would we?"

"I'll have you understand —" Carver began, then fell into a swift silence. Mr. Leggett looked at the doctor, then at Osgood.

"It seems," he said, "that we are being whittled down, one by one. Perhaps this is a matter better held pending until another time."

They all seemed to find this completely agreeable and after hurried goodbyes left the office. The Wind River Kid stared at the closed door, then blew out a relieved breath.

"As a politician," he said, "you don't do bad."

"I told you that I knew this town," Nan said. "That included the bad as well as the good. Dr. Carver's association with the schoolteacher has been a public joke for some time. And in Miles City, the judge finds a certain entertainer at Harrigan's Saloon quite irresistible." She smiled. "Unfortunately, Mr. Osgood didn't linger or I would have reminded him that a man of his age shouldn't chase the female help around the office furniture. And Mr. Leggett's wife is one of Murray Burkhauser's best customers — via the back door, that is. Some say that he has hauled her home in the buggy so often that the horse knows the way."

"Sounds like a pretty low way to fight," the Kid said.

"It's a dirty way," she admitted, "but it is *the* way. Kid, you may not think so, but your way has always been more honorable. Meeting a man face-to-face with a gun has a certain dignity to it. You'll find that missing here. They're all small men, in their souls, and they have to swing a club or anything they can lay their hands on."

"I suppose," he said and went behind his desk to sit down. By stretching his sore legs straight out he found that he could ease the ache.

"Well, I have shopping to do," she said. "And news to gather, especially about the trouble at the mill." Her smile began to brighten her eyes. "And what I really came here for was to invite you to supper. About seven?"

"I'll be there," he said and she went out.

There were no doors in Rindo's Springs

that remained closed to Nan Buckley. She stopped briefly at each business establishment, taking some advertisements, which were the backbone of her paper, and gathering bits of news to enlighten the social-minded. Beneath the hard crust of Rindo's Springs lay the soundings of social activity. There was to be a box lunch at the church, and the school was putting on a play the next week, and the judge had bought his wife a piano, which meant a recital, probably not much musically but certainly important socially.

By mid-afternoon, Nan had a small notebook darkened with scribbling. She stopped at the general store to place her order for the boy's late afternoon delivery; then she started down the street to the print shop.

As she passed the shoemaker's, Cal Runyon entered the street on his bay. She saw him pass, then quite unaccountably, he wheeled around and came back. Nan stopped and Cal Runyon said, "Is there any reason why we can't speak to each other, Nan?"

"None at all," she said. "You're looking fine, Cal. I haven't seen you for months."

"Because I've deliberately avoided you," he said. "Can we talk someplace, Nan?"

"I was going home," she said. "Perhaps

134

you'd like a cup of coffee."

"Thank you, I would." He dismounted and led his horse down the muddy street. At times, when the hitchracks were bare, he could edge close to the boardwalk and walk beside her, but at other times he was forced to walk in the street.

In front of the newspaper office, he tied his horse and entered with her. The typesetter was taking off his apron. He smiled, said goodbye and left. Nan put her notebook on the scarred desk and led the way into her quarters. Cal Runyon paused in the doorway, somewhat ill at ease.

"You haven't changed anything," he said. "But then, you never were one to change much."

"Steady, Nan," she said lightly and began to stoke the fire.

"I went out to see Bess," he said. "You heard about the trouble?"

"The whole town has by this time," she said. "Bess didn't like it, did she?"

He sighed. "That and a lot of other things. Bess and I have reached the end of something, Nan. There's no use trying to fool myself any longer."

She was ladling coffee grounds into the pot; she stopped and turned to face him. "Are you sure, Cal?"

He did not look at her; instead, he studied the design in the rug. "I should have seen it right after her father's funeral. Bess and I have said goodbye."

Her eyes darkened as she searched his face. "Why are you here, Cal? Oh, I know I invited you, but why are you really here?"

"I made a fool's choice, Nan. I just wanted you to know that." He moved his hands aimlessly. "Too bad a man can't do a few things over."

"Cal, we all wish that. It wasn't easy to take, your telling me that it was Bess Jamison you wanted. I think I was angry enough to have shot you gleefully. The hurt was deep because my feelings were deep."

"You don't know how sorry I am," Cal Runyon said softly. "I've regretted that part of it constantly, Nan, the hurting you."

"I've forgiven you," she said, "if that matters."

"It does matter," he said. He stepped toward her, closing the distance almost timidly. "Nan, you're very beautiful. Do you think that we could ever — I mean, have I placed too big a gulf between us?"

"I really don't know," she said. "We'd have to reach, Cal."

And he did reach, for her. She closed her eyes and stood quietly in his arms while he kissed her face and lips. There were no words now; the conversation was carried on in the language all lovers speak — the faint pressure of the hand, the promise of lips on lips.

The delivery boy came to the back door and knocked, but neither of them spoke. Finally the boy set the box of groceries down and went away. Nan Buckley smiled gently and laid her head against Cal Runyon's chest; his hands stroked her bright hair and they stood that way, completely alone.

Promptly at seven, the Wind River Kid locked the door of the office and walked through the twilight toward the newspaper office. The sky was now clear of clouds and a stiff wind husked down the street, rapidly drying the mud. When he came opposite the hotel, he looked up and saw the darkened shape of Will Beau-Haven, injury-locked to his special chair. Beau-Haven's cigar end made a bright glow as he drew on it and his voice floated down. "Drop up sometime."

"I'll do that," the Kid promised and walked on. He turned the corner and at the dark door of the newspaper office, he stopped. Knocking, he waited a moment and when no one answered the door, knocked again. Behind him, at the hitchrail, a horse stomped impatiently and the Kid looked at him.

A streak of light showed under a far door, and by this he knew that Nan was home. Then the streak of light vanished, as though someone had turned the lamp way down. The door opened, and there was enough light remaining to silhouette Nan Buckley as she came toward the dark front, a robe drawn tightly about her. Pressing her face close to the glass, she said, "I don't feel well. I'm sorry about supper."

"That's all right," the Kid said. "I'll drop by tomorrow."

She turned and went back to her quarters. He waited until the far door closed, then started back up town. Two boys raced around the corner nearly knocking the Kid down. He caught one by the arm and looked into a frightened face. "I'm not going to belt you," the Kid said. Almost without reason, he pointed toward the horse tied in front of the newspaper office. "You know who that belongs to?"

One of the boys made a thorough examination. "Looks like Cal Runyon's bay," he said.

The wind seemed to contain more of a

chill than it had a moment before. Slowly the Kid released the boy he held, then gave them each a quarter. Without speaking he walked slowly away. Burkhauser's door was open and very inviting; the Kid stepped onto the porch. From the hotel gallery, Will Beau-Haven called, "Sheriff, you got a minute?"

The Wind River Kid seemed not to hear. The swinging doors gave beneath his hands and he stepped up to the bar. A dozen men sat at tables, drinking and playing cards. A few stood at the bar, but he found a place that looked sufficiently lonesome. The bartender came up, hands busy with his slop rag. The Kid found a dollar and laid it down. "Will that buy pretty good stuff?"

"Damn good," the man said and produced a bottle.

He took it and put it under his coat as though he were half-ashamed to be seen with it in public. At the sheriff's office, he let himself in and locked the door behind him. The place was dark and he put a match to the lamp, then went into his own room and sat down on the bed.

Placing the bottle on the floor between his feet, he sat hunched over, his face mirroring his gray thoughts. He was not the sort of man who jumped to a hasty conclusion without looking at all the facts, but this time his emotions pulled him into a quick judgment. He placed none of the blame on Nan Buckley; Cal Runyon was the center of the Kid's bitter thoughts.

A rational portion of his mind told him that it was none of his business; Nan had already told him about Runyon and if he had been fool enough to believe all the fire was out, then he had no one to blame but himself. Yet too many factors entered into the computation, tilting it completely off the scale. There were those years when the wrong business or the wrong friends had slammed doors in his face, coupled with a certain sensitivity that had always troubled him. These factors added to the belief that he had at last shed his past served to drive the bitterness deeper.

Since the Wind River Kid was not much different from other men who found facing themselves much more difficult than facing danger, uncorking the bottle of whiskey was the next logical step. And he took it.

He was not a sociable drinker and he never claimed to be. Whiskey was akin to a blow on the head; it made him forget. Yet he could not do that as easily as he thought. When the bottle was half-gone, all the Kid had gained was a growing anger and increasing dizziness.

Deserting the bottle, he returned to the street. Burkhauser's place still worked hard to make itself the liveliest in town, but the Kid had little interest there. His step was unsteady, partly from his sore leg, partly due to the whiskey. But his aches seemed to have diminished, and he persuaded himself that he felt fine.

Turning toward the newspaper office, he saw that Cal Runyon's bay still stood three-footed at the hitchrack. His impulse was to bang on the door and demand an opportunity to avenge a lady's honor, but even drunk he could see how damned silly that would look.

Waiting seemed to be his best course of action so he eased into the bakery doorway where the wind did not bite so much. Time scuffed its feet and he checked his watch at what seemed to be half-hour intervals but were actually only five-minute breaks. An eternity later, the front door of the newspaper office opened and Cal Runyon stepped out, adjusting his hat to his head.

When Runyon stepped under the hitchrail, the Kid eased out of the doorway. "Hold on there," he said softly.

Runyon turned about. He bent forward to peer through the darkness. "Sheriff? That you? What the devil you doing lurking in doorways?"

"Waiting for you," the Kid said flatly. He stepped toward Runyon and nearly stumbled.

Runyon retied the reins and came to the boardwalk. "You drunk?" He stepped close and then said, "By God, you've been hitting it all right. What's got into you, man?"

"You," the Kid said. He tried to give Runyon a shove backward and only succeeded in pushing himself off balance. "We got something to settle, we have."

"What the devil are you —" Cal Runyon stopped. "Oh, I see." He raised a hand and wiped his mouth. "I don't suppose you'd listen to sense."

"That's right," the Kid said. "She smiled at me, Cal. Treated me like a human being who was as good as the next man." He laughed bitterly. "Then you had to come along and make her as cheap and ugly as all the others I've known."

"Did I do all that?" Runyon asked softly. "Kid, I loved her long before you ever saw her."

"You had a woman," the Kid pointed out. "What do you do, change your mind every week?"

Cal Runyon stepped back under the

142

hitchrack, his fingers untying the reins. "I don't have to listen to that," he said. "Sober up, Kid; then we'll talk."

"Then we'll fight," the Kid said stubbornly. "We're going to fight, Cal."

"I won't pick it," he said. "Come around tomorrow, sober, and then if you still want to fight, I might accommodate you."

"There's no time like now," the Kid said and stepped toward Runyon who waited calmly on the other side of the hitchrack.

When the Kid drew within range, he uncorked a punch meant to be a scorcher, but Runyon ducked it easily. He then hooked the Kid's shirt front with his hands, yanked hard and brought the hitchrail hard against the Kid's stomach. With flailing arms and legs, the Kid went over. He struck the road on all fours as Nan Buckley opened the front door.

"Cal, you forgot to —" She saw the Kid getting up. "What are you doing down there?"

With the solidness of the hitchrack to help him, the Kid got to his feet. Nan stepped toward him, but stopped when Cal Runyon said, "He's got a mad on, Nan. Let him work it off."

"He's been drinking," Nan said, surprised. "Don't hurt him, Cal."

This detached conversation riled the Kid to a fever anger. His charge took Runyon completely by surprise and both men slammed into the horse's hip. Swinging, the horse lashed out with his hind feet and both men escaped by a narrow margin. Downed, Runyon and the Kid rolled beneath the horse, then Runyon came up on the other side, his hands lifting the Kid clear. As the Kid came to his feet he whipped his fist around and hit Cal Runyon flush in the mouth, driving him back.

Even drunk, the Wind River Kid was a better fighter than most men, and Runyon saw this too late. Runyon tried to close, to grab one of the Kid's arms, and took a crack over the eye that split skin, then another that opened his upper lip.

"Cal," Nan shouted, "Cal, can't you grab him?"

"Like a — damned eel," Runyon said, trying to get the Kid's arms pinned down.

There was kindness in Runyon, and this defeated him from the start, for there was nothing but anger in the Kid, anger and a childish desire to even off some of the hurt. Finally Runyon tired of taking this and tried to hit the Kid. He landed a weak blow to the Kid's cheek, but the power was lost when the Kid rolled away.

Runyon took a raking blow across the bridge of his nose and swore. Then, when all else failed, he tried to wrestle his way out of it, hoping that the Kid's intoxication would make him clumsy. But the exercise, the release of anger had sobered the Kid, and he grabbed Runyon around the neck and held him while he flailed him in the face with his fist. This angered Cal Runyon, wiped away his kind intent, but he found a purpose too late, because the Wind River Kid had him on the run, had him on the defensive.

The Kid punched with machine precision, and he hit hard, quickly. Finally Runyon backed away completely and raised a hand to his bloody face. He was nearly out of breath, and quite weary. "Wait," he gasped. "You've licked me — if that's what you — want."

Runyon pawed at the mud clinging to his clothes, mud he had picked up rolling beneath the horse's feet. His glance touched Nan Buckley, a glance filled with apology.

Yet it was the Kid who apologized. "Sorry I butted in," he said and turned away.

"Kid! Wait!"

"Let him go," Runyon said softly. "Talk won't change anything, Nan."

"How did he — ?"

"My horse, I guess," Runyon said. "He was waiting for me when I came out.'

Nan pulled her robe tighter about her. "What have we done, Cal? To ourselves and to him?"

"Something we can't undo," he said and mounted. "Get inside before someone sees you."

"Yes," she said, so softly that he could barely hear her. "Before someone sees me. Our kind has to have the darkness, isn't that right, Cal?"

"You'll feel better about it in the morning," he said.

She looked steadily at him for a moment, then went inside, shutting the door. Runyon hesitated a moment, then turned his horse down the street toward the jail. A drunk reeled out of Burkhauser's as he passed, hailing loudly, but Runyon ignored him and went on. Dismounting before the jail, he tied his horse and went inside.

The Wind River Kid was in his small room, stripped to his underwear. He had filled a wooden tub with water and was methodically washing his clothes. When Runyon stopped in the doorway, the Kid glanced at him, then went back to his work.

"I don't like being dirty," he said softly.

"None of us do," Runyon said. "But it

isn't long after we're born that we start rolling in it." He took a cigar from his pocket, then offered one to the Kid, who shook his head. "Kid, is this the end of this between us? Or are we going to tangle again?"

"It's the end," the Kid said. The sounds from Burkhauser's drifted fitfully through the walls, and a heavy wagon trundled down the street, building a brief racket. "There's an old pair of jeans and a shirt hanging in the other room," he said. "Mind getting them?"

"Sure," Runyon said. He went out and a moment later came back, laying the clothes on the bed. He sat down and observed the Kid carefully. "You like Nan, huh?"

"She seemed different," the Kid said.

"Different?" Runyon shook his head. "That's the trouble with men, Kid. The one woman for them always seems different from the others. They're not. We're not. All the same, Kid. All born the same way, and most of us die the same, as disappointed as the next man." He paused to examine the cigar ash. "People are always apologizing for what they do," he went on. "What I'm trying to get across to you, Kid, is that neither Nan nor I have to apologize for being human."

"All right!" the Kid shouted. "All right,

147

you made your damn point. Now leave me alone."

Cal Runyon blew out a thin cloud of cigar smoke, then stood up. "You think Nan's sure to end in perdition, don't you?"

"What difference does it make to me? She made her choice."

"Yes," Runyon said, "she did, and I think not too good a one."

He walked out of the small room and into the main office. From down, the street came the rattle of a wagon, the snap and jingle of harness. Curious, he stepped to the door for his look.

The darkness kept him from a full recognition until the wagon stopped in front of the jail. From the high seat, Ben Colfax said, "Been out to the mill, Cal. Got some trouble here."

Runyon stepped to the boardwalk, peered up at the canvas-wrapped man atop the load. "He dead?"

"Plumb dead." Ben Colfax took off his hat and ran his fingers through his hair. "This is real trouble. The new sheriff around?"

"Kid!" Runyon turned toward the interior of the office, but the Kid was on his way. He brushed past Runyon, hopped onto the wagon and peeled back an edge of the canvas. The combination of night and a bloody face was not enough to shroud the man's identity; he was the same man who had quarreled at the tie mill.

Runyon too had his look, then spoke briefly to Ben Colfax. "Go get the doctor."

"Hell, he likes his sleep," Colfax said. "In the morning's time enough —"

"Damn it, I said go get him. This is Bess Jamison's man. In the morning we may have a full-scale shooting war on our hands over this."

7

While Ben Colfax went for a doctor, the Kid returned to his back room, stoked the fire beneath the coffee pot, and when it was hot, drank several cups. Cal Runyon perched on the edge of the cot, gloomily turning the room dense with his cigar. The coffee, he noticed, seemed to improve the Kid's disposition, neutralizing the remaining effects of the alcohol.

Ben Colfax came back and hurried inside. He took a lantern out of the closet and lighted it so that Dr. Carver could make a preliminary examination before the dead man was moved. The Kid and Cal Runyon came to the front door and stood there.

"Exactly what happened?" the Kid asked. Colfax looked around, then climbed down off the load. He cuffed his hat to the back of his head, looked at Cal Runyon, then motioned toward the office with his hand.

They went in and the Kid closed the door.

"We got to the railroad siding," Colfax said. "I got down first and went around to the other side of the wagon. There was a shot and he just crumpled over."

"Did you see who it was?" Cal Runyon asked.

Ben Colfax looked at him briefly, then nodded. "Can't be sure, you understand, seein' as how it was dark and all. But he either had on a white shirt, or his arm was bandaged."

"Are you saying it was Pete?" Runyon snapped.

"Said I wasn't sure," Colfax repeated.

Dr. Carver stepped inside. "I'll have him taken to my house if it's all right with you, sheriff."

"Go ahead." After Carver closed the door, the Kid faced Ben Colfax. "Ben, how sure are you that Pete fired that shot?"

Colfax slapped his hands together. "Thunderation, how can I be sure? I only said it could have been Pete; he had his arm bandaged. And Pete had reason enough; everyone knows how he nurses a grudge. Ask Cal. The fight went sour on him, didn't it?"

"That's all true enough," Runyon admitted. "We'd better talk to Pete."

"You stay here, Ben," the Kid said. He

started for the back room to get his gun, then recalled that it had slipped out of his holster and was now lying in the mud in front of Nan's newspaper office. To Ben he said, "Lend me your pistol."

There was a moment's caution in Ben Colfax' eyes, then he unbuckled the gun-belt and handed it over. "You going to arrest Pete?" Colfax asked.

"If there's need for it," the Kid said. He opened the door and then allowed Cal Runyon to step out ahead of him. They walked together toward the company buildings. Finally the Kid said, "What do you think, Cal? Do you believe Pete's the kind of man who'd pot someone off a wagon?"

"No," Runyon said flatly. "I've known him awhile. He takes his fights to a man's face. He's tough and quarrelsome, but he settles things openly."

"If what Ben says is true, then Pete changed his habits."

"I hate to think so, Kid. Too many things are changing around here."

"You're Ben's friend, aren't you? You want me to believe him, don't you?"

"I trust Ben," Runyon said. "You make up your own mind."

"That's my habit."

"I think you look at things too closely,"

Runyon said.

They walked the rest of the way in silence. The main gate guard admitted them and they went to the main bunkhouse. Twenty minutes later, both men were heading back for the sheriff's office, for a few questions revealed that neither Pete nor his horse were where they should be, and the company hostler recalled that Pete had come straight from the doctor, saddled up and ridden out.

When the Kid and Runyon reached the side street on which Judge Richmond lived, the Kid stopped. "I'm going to get a warrant for Pete's arrest."

"My horse is still tied in front of the jail. I'll wait for you there and go with you."

"All right. See that mine is saddled and waiting." He walked away and a moment later turned into the dark path leading toward the judge's house. The place was dark but the Kid pounded on the door until a lamp was lit upstairs and a head showed at a window.

"Who the devil's down there and what do you want at this hour?"

"It's the sheriff," the Kid said. "Open up, judge. There's been an accident."

The window banged shut and a moment later a blob of light descended the stairs and a shadow darkened the other side of the glass-paneled door. Richmond flung it open and the Kid stepped inside. The judge was in his nightshirt, a heavy displeasure mottling his face.

"Couldn't this have waited until morning?" he asked.

"One of Bess Jamison's men has been killed," the Kid said.

"Hell, that can wait until morning."

"Not if you want to prevent a war," the Kid pointed out. "I have enough evidence against a man to go after him. If I can put him in jail before Bess Jamison gets here with her crowd, she'll have to admit that the law isn't all Cadmus Rindo's."

"One of Rindo's men did it?"

"Looks that way," the Kid said. "I want you to issue a warrant for Pete Davis."

"Hmmm," Richmond said, rubbing his face. "We'd best go sure and easy there, sheriff. It won't do to rile Rindo in order to keep from riling Bess Jamison."

"I said I had some evidence," the Kid said. He smiled without humor. "Judge, there's a warrant out for me on even less evidence."

The judge puffed his cheeks and sighed, then went to his desk and filled out the proper papers. He handed them over and said, "This can trigger off a lot of trouble."

"And a lot more if nothing's done about

it," the Kid said. He left without further delay and cut toward the jail. Cal Runyon was there, puffing on a fresh cigar, his face pinched with concern. Ben Colfax had his feet elevated to the desk top, a satisfied expression on his face.

When the Kid stepped inside, Colfax said, "Told you that you'd need me, Kid." He chuckled. "I'm an old fire-horse that hears the bell."

"Then enjoy the ringing," the Kid said. He motioned toward the door. "Come on, I want to lock up."

This was as close to being thrown out as a man could get without actually being tossed. Colfax looked angry and offended and full of argument. "This the thanks a man gets?"

"Thanks for what? Come on. We've got to go."

Colfax stood up and moved toward the door. "You taking him, why not take me? Been a lawman all my life and I could give you a lot of points."

"And I've been dodging lawmen," the Kid said. He waited until Runyon stepped out, then locked the door. Ben Colfax stood on the boardwalk, looking for a wedge to open a new argument, but the Kid didn't give him any. Runyon had brought up his horse and he stepped into the saddle. When Runyon swung up, the Kid said, "Go home and go to bed, Ben. I'm not going to make you a deputy."

"You may be sorry for that," Colfax said and shuffled off into the night.

Cal Runyon's frown was deep. "He meant well, Kid. Probably could have been a help."

"I don't want him around," the Kid said and turned his horse out of town.

"You got something against him?"

"I don't trust a thief," the Kid said flatly. "And Ben Colfax is a thief."

For a moment, Runyon clung to silence while he phrased words in his mind. "Kid, I hope you can prove that."

"Do I have to?" He looked squarely at Runyon. "He stole from me and that's all the proof I need."

The flat finality in the Kid's voice froze any further argument Cal Runyon might have had, and they settled down to the ride. The wind snapped along with its chill, but the clear sky held no promise of rain.

There was a lot to learn about the Wind River Kid, Runyon decided, and he discovered a few things during the three-hour ride. The Kid was at home in this element, and he possessed an uncanny sense of direction. In a short time he gauged the fall and rise of the land, and insisted upon leaving the road to cut through the timbered sections. As though guided by an extra perception, he sought out the small, back trails, the shortcuts, and after shaving a half-hour off the normal time, stopped on a high ridge and looked down on the railroad terminus.

Cal Runyon said, "I never knew this way, Kid."

"Pete did," the Kid said. "Any man who's moved around a lot would have taken the shortcut over the mountain instead of riding around it." He rapped his heels against the horse's flanks and started down, wending his way through the avenues of tall timber. The ground was wet and soggy and they made no sounds at all, except for the occasional snapping of a dead branch or the whisper of pressing through light brush. The forest was ink-dark, yet the Kid made no mistakes. To Runyon it seemed that this man had traveled this trail many times, yet he knew that the Kid was a stranger to it.

The railroad terminal did business on a twenty-four-hour basis. The roundhouse was lighted and switchers puffed back and forth on the siding, shuffling empties and strings of loaded cars. A railroad-owned town sat off to the right beneath the crouching brow of a high bluff. The Kid slanted down off the ridge and once he hit the flats, ignored the yard section and rode into the town. Runyon wanted to stop, but the Kid shook his head and rode the length of the street. The buildings were all framed with lumber sawed at Rindo's mill, and all were painted an identical tan. A saloon and yard foreman's hotel sat on opposite corners, both brightly lighted. The rest of the town was dark, but the Kid wasn't interested in the buildings. His attention was focused on the horses standing nose-in at the hitch-racks. He rode slowly down one side of the street, then turned and came back on the other.

To Runyon, he said, "You would recognize the horse, wouldn't you?"

"A dun gelding," Runyon said.

"If you see it, you'll be sure to mention it, won't you?"

Runyon gave him an offended stare. "I don't hide my men, Kid. Get that notion out of your head."

The gelding was found tied in front of the saloon. The Kid and Runyon tied up along-side and stood for a moment on the board-walk. "Are you carrying a gun?" the Kid asked.

"Yes," Runyon admitted.

"Let me have it." He held out his hand and waited.

"Just what is this? Hell, I'm a grown man; I can handle it."

"Come on, Cal. Hand it over."

Reluctantly, Runyon reached beneath his coat and snapped his gun free of a shoulder holster. It was a .38 Smith & Wesson and the Kid broke it open, spilling the cartridges before handing it back. Runyon resettled the pistol beneath his armpit. "What did you think I was going to do, shoot you in the back?"

"I don't want you shooting anyone," the Kid said, starting for the saloon porch. He paused to look over the louvered doors, then went inside, Runyon following a pace behind. A quick survey of the bar told him that Pete Davis was not there; then he saw the man sitting in the far corner, a half-filled beer stein before him.

Moving between the tables, the Kid flanked him, then suddenly scraped a chair aside and sat down across from the man. Pete Davis looked up slowly and said, "Been expecting you." His glance found Cal Runyon. "You believe I did it?"

"I don't know what to believe, Pete." Cal remained standing.

"Well, I didn't do it," Pete said flatly. He locked eyes with the Kid. "You don't believe that, do you?"

"You're here. Your gun's gone. And Ben Colfax said he thought he saw you at the time Bess's man was shot."

"If Colfax says I shot him, then he's a liar." Pete Davis patted his stomach. "And my gun's here, under my coat."

"If you didn't kill him," Runyon asked, "then who did?"

"I don't know," Pete said flatly. "After I left the doc's place, I got to thinking, so I saddled up and came here, meaning to finish what I started without having the law interfere." He looked squarely at the Kid. "I waited around and finally saw the wagon come into the siding. Then there was a shot and Ben Colfax was yelling about someone being killed."

"You saw all this?" Runyon asked.

"Sure, but from a distance." Davis paused to drink some of his beer. "I'm not a fool; I knew this would look bad for me. That's why I waited here instead of lighting out. Besides, Kid, we ain't settled our little difference yet."

"You'll have to come back with me," the Kid said softly.

Davis raised his eyes. "To jail?"

"There'll have to be a trial," the Kid said. "That's the law, Pete."

"They'll hang me." He shook his head. "I

can't take the chance."

"You'll have to take it," the Kid said. "Drink the rest of your beer and let's go, Pete. There's no sense trying to draw against me now."

Davis glanced at Runyon. "You going to help him take me back?"

"He's the law," Cal Runyon said. "And his way's best, Pete."

"Not for me it ain't. If a jury don't convict me, Bess's bunch will find some way to get to me." He placed his hands flat on the table. "I've heard plenty about the Wind River Kid, but I'll take a chance."

"You're acting like a fool!" Runyon said.

"Stay out of this, Cal," the Kid said. He stood up slowly. "Let's go, Pete." With great clarity, the Wind River Kid realized that he did not want to kill this man, but if he was forced to shoot, it would have to be clean and for keeps. Watching Pete Davis, the Kid understood that this man was also tired and wanted out, only he couldn't put his pride aside, and because of that there would be no way out.

Yet for a heartbeat it seemed that Pete was going to obey, but then Pete rammed forward with his shoulder, upset the table, and drew his gun. He was a practiced man, skilled, confident that his speed and accuracy were superior to all others.

Cal Runyon jumped back and the Kid grabbed the table as it spun toward him and hoisted it in front of him as Pete Davis let the hammer slide from under his thumb. The bullet puckered the wood, passed through with a rending of slivers, then imbedded in the far wall. Men boiled to their feet, colliding with each other in their haste to get down and out of the line of fire.

Cal Runyon yelled a warning to the Kid, who needed none. Pete was recocking his gun, leveling it, sighting more carefully this time. The Kid knew that there would be no way to take Pete now, and that the table was not stout enough to stop a bullet.

His palm popped against the slick butt as he swept the gun up with tremendous speed, cocking, whipping it waist high, firing in one, smooth, uninterrupted motion. The pistol recoiled in his hand and he held it that way, muzzle up-tilted, powdersmoke a haze about him. Pete whirled half around, the gun falling from his relaxed fingers. Then he settled face down. The saloon was strangely silent and the Kid put his gun away.

"It had to be a killing shot," he said, as if apologizing to the fallen man.

"We know that," Cal Runyon said.

Boots thrashed across the porch, and a big man in a derby hat came in. He was armed with a sawed-off shotgun and a long billy-club. Punching and jabbing his way through the crowd, he had his look at Pete Davis, then turned to the Kid. "I'm Cassidy, the railroad marshal. Who're you?" His glance touched the badge.

"Jim Onart, the sheriff at Rindo's Springs."

"I'll have to make a report," Cassidy said, "since it happened here. You want to come over to the office?"

"Sure."

"I'll stay and put Pete on his horse so we can take him back," Runyon said.

The Kid nodded and followed Cassidy through the crowd. Once on the street, Cassidy said, "I try to keep the desperadoes out of this town. He was a bad one, huh?"

"No, just a man who had to do everything the hard way," the Kid said.

The marshal's office was on the main thoroughfare and they went inside. Another man was there, a tall man in his late thirties. He wore a neat, dark suit and a pearl-handled Colt slung low against his thigh. When Cassidy and the Kid stepped inside, this man stood up. "Marshal?"

"I'm the marshal," Cassidy said. "What

can I do for you?"

The man exposed his left cuff, revealing a small, crescent-shaped badge. "I'm Boomhauer, United States marshal."

"Glad to know you," Cassidy said, offering his hand. "You must have come in on the 11:36 train." He turned to the Kid. "This is the sheriff from Rindo's Springs."

"A pleasure," Boomhauer said, shaking the Kid's hand. Boomhauer had a bland face, the kind usually associated with a careful businessman. His hair was sandy and he had a tawny mustache that drooped past the ends of his lips. "Rindo's Springs, you say? Coincidence, but that's my destination. Perhaps we could ride back together."

"If you don't mind the company of a dead man," the Kid said. He gave Cassidy his attention, yet regarded Boomhauer furtively when the marshal was not looking. Cassidy was at his desk, pen in hand. "What was the dead man's name, sheriff?"

The Kid gave him the facts and Cassidy wrote every bit of it down. Just as he finished, Cal Runyon came in. To the Kid he said, "I got Pete wrapped in a canvas and tied to his horse."

"You want to get some sleep before you start back? Be daylight in another hour."

"I'm in no rush," Runyon said. "If you

want me, I'll be bunked down at the stable." He went out and the Kid went to the door, there pausing.

"If that's all, Cassidy, I think I'll find something to eat."

"There's an all-night dining room at the hotel," Cassidy said.

Boomhauer reached down and retrieved a small satchel. "Sheriff," he said, "if you have no objection, I'll join you."

For an instant the Kid surveyed him critically, then shrugged. With Boomhauer walking beside him, the Kid headed back for the saloon. "Trouble is always unpleasant," Boomhauer said, his voice mild and pleasant. "Been with the law long?"

"I've been associated with it for a few years," the Kid admitted. He stepped into the bar and collared the bartender. "Did you pick up that fella's gun?"

"Got it right here," he said and handed it over.

"Evidence," the Kid said and slipped it into his waistband. He turned and went out, Boomhauer at his heels. Across the street, in the hotel dining room, the Kid and Boomhauer ordered a big meal, then settled back to wait for it.

To Boomhauer the Kid said "Rindo's Springs is your destination, you say?"

"Yes." He brought out a yellow telegram and spread it on the table. "Our office in The Dalles received this."

The telegram read:

IF YOU ARE STILL LOOKING FOR THE WIND RIVER KID COME TO RINDO'S SPRINGS.

"We checked immediately with the Arizona marshal's office and there is a warrant out for this man. Have you seen him around your town?"

All men find strangeness in discussing themselves as a separate entity, and the Kid had to beat down this uneasiness before he could speak. "You sure this isn't some kind of a joke?"

Boomhauer's shoulders rose and fell. "Sheriff, we never treat a warrant like a joke." He smiled. "You know that we don't try men. We only arrest them."

"What about a description? A picture?"

"No pictures," Boomhauer said. "And the description fits at least ten men I know." The waiter brought their meal and all conversation ground to a halt while appetites were blunted.

"I suppose you'll want to look the town over," the Kid said, forcing an easiness into his voice.

"Routine," Boomhauer said. "Likely you're right; it's a joke." Then his eyelids pulled together slightly. "But again, why would anyone send a telegram? It's never happened before."

"Well, good luck with your manhunt," the Wind River Kid said.

"I've been hoping I won't find him at all," Boomhauer said, quite seriously. "You see, the Wind River Kid isn't exactly what I call a criminal. True, he's fast with a gun and he's left a few stretched out behind him, but those were clearly self-defense, according to reliable witnesses. Unfortunately, the Kid fought on the wrong side of a range war. Now a politically rotten sheriff has a warrant slapped on him." He paused to drink some of his coffee. "Listening to you make that report to Cassidy started me thinking. If I meet the Wind River Kid, I'll have to arrest him, just like you had to arrest this Pete What's-His-Name. The Kid isn't the kind who'll go back to a crooked jury and a paid-off judge." Boomhauer's voice softened. "I'll likely have to draw on him, and then there'll be another dead man."

"Maybe you," the Kid said.

"Maybe, but I've drawn on men before.

Good men." He shrugged again, and attacked his apple pie. "But we're talking about the future, and something that might never happen."

"But if it does?"

Boomhauer paused, looking steadily at the Wind River Kid. "Then I'll have to do what you did. That's the regrettable part of our job, isn't it?"

Through the remainder of the meal they talked of other things, and the Kid found much in Wade Boomhauer to admire. The man had been around, and always on the right side of the law. He understood killers and governors with equal clarity, and shading all of his opinions was a fine sense of responsibility and justice.

The Kid paid for the meal and walked to the stable. He talked the hostler out of a horse for Boomhauer, then found Cal Runyon and woke him. Mounted, they left the railroad town and drove for the mountain road that led back to Rindo's Springs.

The day was dull and gray at first, then the sun came out, sucking steam from the earth until it drifted like thick wood smoke. By nine o'clock they shed their coats, and at ten stopped to rest their horses.

Runyon had introduced himself earlier, so he fell into conversation with Wade Boomhauer now. "You after a man?" he asked. He found spare cigars and passed them around.

While taking his light, Boomhauer said "Got word — the Wind River Kid — was in your town."

Cal Runyon simply stared, then caught himself. He avoided a direct look at the Kid. "Sounds like a crank's work. I know just about everyone in Rindo's Springs."

"Probably so," Boomhauer said, puffing gently on his cigar. "Still, I'll have to check it out."

The Kid indicated that he was ready to mount, but he and Cal Runyon held back, letting Boomhauer go on ahead out of earshot. "Kid, what the hell you going to do? When he starts asking questions, the word will be out."

"There's no hiding it," the Kid admired.

"There's one way," Runyon said softly. "Rindo still controls the town. If I say so, no one will dare open his mouth."

"That wouldn't shut up all of them." The Kid sighed. "Well, it had to happen and now that it has, I really don't mind it."

"You're a strange one," Runyon said and then pushed forward to side Boomhauer.

8

The Kid took Pete Davis' body to Dr. Carver's house and carried it into his small operating room.

Looking around, Carver said dryly, "My, but business has picked up since you came to town."

The Kid frowned. "That's not funny."

"Well," Carver said, swinging around, "you're in a bad mood!" He opened the canvas covering Pete Davis and examined the bullet hole. "Dead center. This from the hip?" He caught the Kid's scowl and raised his hand. "All right, all right. Just a scientific question."

"Did you take the bullet out of the teamster?" the Kid asked.

"Take all the bullets out," Carver boasted. "Thorough, that's the way I work. You want to see it?" He got a small jar out of a cupboard and opened it. Five bullets lay in his palm, each neatly tagged. "A few of these were before your arrival," he said. "This one came out of Bess Jamison's father." He picked up another. "Here's the one you want."

The Wind River Kid looked at it carefully, then slipped Pete's gun out of his waistband. He read the stamping on the barrel: Colt Single Action Army .45.

"Something wrong?" Carver asked, reading correctly the puzzled expression on the Kid's face.

"Are you sure you took this one out of the teamster?"

"Sure, I'm sure. What's the matter?"

"The slug is from an old .44 American. Notice how light it is? No other .44 is that light. The .44 American is getting pretty rare as a handgun load. Pete's gun is a .45 Colt."

"Then Pete didn't kill —" Carver paused to stroke his chin. "Say, that puts a different head on the beer, don't it?"

"Yes, and you keep it under your hat," the Kid said, turning toward the door.

"You want to see the bullet I'll take out of Pete?"

"No," the Kid said. "I know who put that one there."

He let himself out and walked slowly toward the center of town. Until now there had been no doubt in the Kid's mind that he had shot the guilty man; the way Pete had bolted had convinced him. But now all that vanished like a patch of early morning fog; the physical evidence of the mismated bullets was simple and undeniable. Since bullets were his business, he thought instantly of the possibilities of shooting .44 American loads in a .45. Of course accuracy went to hell, but this had been done before with confusing results. Two things knocked this possibility out as far as the Kid was concerned. First, Pete would have had to do the shooting at over twenty yards and at night; a .44 fired in a .45 was not accurate enough for that. And secondly, the .44 taken from the teamster had well-set rifling marks; that couldn't happen in an oversize barrel.

As the Kid passed the hotel, the clerk saw him and beckoned him in. "Sheriff," he said, "Mr. Beau-Haven told me that if I saw you, to ask you to step up. He wants to see you."

"All right."

"Straight up the stairs and first door to your right."

With a nod, the Kid mounted the steps, listening to them squeak beneath his weight. At the proper door he knocked, then listened to tapping heels approach. When the door opened, Grace Beau-Haven said,

"Won't you come in, sheriff? My husband is taking the air on the upper gallery."

She took the Kid's hat and placed it on the sideboard. He followed her through two lavishly decorated rooms. Double doors opened onto the railed gallery overlooking Rindo's Springs. Will Beau-Haven sat in his special-built chair, a robe wrapped about his useless legs.

"This is the sheriff, dear," she said. "My husband, Will."

The Kid shook hands briefly with Will Beau-Haven, then sat down when offered one of the chairs. Grace lingered by her husband, her hands gentle on his shoulders. Her face was composed and her eyes held a slightly vacant expression, as though her mind were busy elsewhere. The Kid had noticed instantly her purposeful drabness. He knew it was not an accident, for she wore rice powder to disguise the natural radiant color of her skin. Her dress was a dark gray with only twin ribbons of black trim bisecting the bodice. And the dress was loosely fit, almost shapeless. Grace Beau-Haven, he observed, was a neat woman. Her hair, although severely dressed, was burnished smooth, and she took pride in her hands. Such a woman, he deduced, would not wear a misfit dress unless she had a definite reason, and he could only guess at what it might be.

"Going to rain again," Will Beau-Haven observed. "You notice how muddy-looking it was at dawn?"

"I'm a poor weather prophet," the Kid said.

"Hard for me to ignore it. Get my shooting pains when the weather changes." He canted his head to look at his wife. "How about some fresh coffee, Grace?"

"Tonic for you," she said. "But I'll fix the sheriff some."

When she went inside, Will Beau-Haven glanced at the Kid. "New man in town. Understand he's the federal law."

"Boomhauer. Nice fella."

"Not when he finds out who you are," Will Beau-Haven said. "How long do you think you can keep it from him?"

"I never treated it like it was a contest," the Kid said.

"May be a shooting contest when he finds out." He looked carefully at the Wind River Kid. "I'll have a good seat, won't I? The best in town. I sit here, day in, day out, looking down, seeing everything that's worth seeing. Don't get a chance to tell what I see, though. People are too busy to talk to a cripple." He paused and looked down toward the street, studying Burkhauser's place. "I see everything that goes on over there. You take that gap between Burkhauser's and the general store; used to be a door there, but it's been boarded up for six months now. Richmond, Colfax and Doc Carver used to use that door regular, then they suddenly stopped. Been bothering me, not knowing why." He chuckled. "Sheriff, how much would you charge me to watch all night and see what goes on in that gap?"

"Something going on?" the Kid asked softly.

"You take a look at all the other gaps between all the other buildings in town. Filled up with bottles and junk. But look across the street. That gap's kept clean. Make you wonder?"

"Damned if it don't," the Kid said. He turned his head at a slight sound and found Grace Beau-Haven standing there with a tray. Her expression was composed and neutral when she poured the coffee. He added sugar and canned milk, then sat with the cup nestled in his hands.

"Quite a town, Rindo's Springs," Beau-Haven said, as though picking up a conversational thread dropped when his wife came back. "A lot goes on down there. Men pulling against each other, planning to do better — or do worse, which a man can do easy enough all the while he thinks he's doing better." He sighed and drank the tonic she handed him. Then he made a face and set the empty glass aside. "Not many towns like this one, where one man made it and keeps it alive." He waved his hands at the street. "There are men walking around down there just waiting for the old man to die so they can swoop in and gobble up what he's spent a lifetime building. Damn fools! Once they begin fighting over what the other man has, they'll lose everything."

"A man has to stand or fall by himself," the Wind River Kid said. "You can't blame people for wanting that right."

Will Beau-Haven laughed, then leaned forward and tapped the Kid's knee with his finger. "Rindo built all this and picked nearly every man who lives here. That's what I said, picked. Hand-picked." He sagged back. "Maybe it was a kind of cruel joke he played on everyone, or maybe it was because he felt he had to do it."

"You've talked this into quite a thing," the Kid said.

"Talk?" Beau-Haven laughed. "Man, live here. Get to know these people. Look at them. Examine them carefully. They're all imperfect specimens."

"Hell, we all are."

Beau-Haven shook his head vigorously. "Not the way I mean. Nearly every man here is a misfit. Unable to hold himself up, and yet unable to admit it to himself. Rindo looked for that weakness when he allowed them to settle here. Take myself. I was just a muleskinner until I got crippled. Rindo gave me a share in this place because I was useless for anything else."

The Wind River Kid looked at Grace Beau-Haven, opening his mouth to ask her if she approved of this view, but the words failed to come out. She was sitting perfectly straight, her eyes fixed on some inward scene. She appeared to be in a trance.

"She gets like that," Beau-Haven said. "Let her alone and she'll be all right. Lord knows what she dreams about." He took the Kid's sleeve and shook it. "There's something wrong with every man in this town. Nan Buckley's father came here in disgrace. Burkhauser was a gambler whose only talent was dealing off the bottom of the deck. Ben Colfax was nothing, just a man who'd been a deputy and lacked the brains for anything better. I could go on, but it would be the same. That's why we sit around hating Cadmus Rindo, because we know what we are and that we'll never be any better no matter how many chances we have. Kid, you never win a man's heart by sharing your wealth with him. But you show him your weakness and fear and he'll be a friend."

"It seems that I'm well qualified for Rindo's Springs," the Kid said dryly.

"You've already been signed up and initiated," Beau-Haven said.

The Kid finished his coffee in silence while Beau-Haven studied the street. Perhaps, the Kid decided, there was some truth in this bitter judgment, and in the years to come, he might also realize that there would never be anything better. But youth had hope, and he was still young, no matter how worn-out he might feel at times.

When he stood up, Grace Beau-Haven blinked and said, "Leaving? Why, it seems that you only just came."

The Kid said goodbye and Grace Beau-Haven walked with him to the door. "You musn't mind Will," she said. "He's very bitter."

"And you?"

Her eyes became softly warm and dreamy. "We all have our own little worlds, sheriff."

He gave her a brief nod, placed his hat carefully on his head and went down the stairs. As he entered the lobby, the clerk signaled him over. "The marshal who came into town with you," the clerk said, "has number eight. Last room, street side, on this floor."

"Thanks," the Kid said, turning away.

"Oh, sheriff." The Kid turned back. "Miss Buckley's waiting." He nodded toward a sheltered corner and following his eyes, the Kid saw Nan sitting in one of the heavy leather chairs.

Stepping up to her, the Kid said, "I made a big fool of myself last night."

"I didn't come here to point that out," she said. "Kid, what are you going to do about this U. S. marshal?"

He shrugged. "What do you expect me to do?"

"He's catching up on his sleep now," she said, "but then he'll start asking questions. He's bound to find out."

"It's my problem, not yours."

He deliberately closed her out, and her pride made her chin come up. "Of course," she said softly. "I'm sorry I meddled." Quickly, before he could stop her, she got up and walked out.

The Kid silently cursed himself for being a fool, yet his pride gave him little choice. Before, when observing two people in love, he had always considered it amusing when they flung these shaded ultimatums at each other, but now the humor vanished. This thought brought him up short; a man's first realization that he is at last in love is rather shattering.

His anger at her was very understandable now, for it had been a jealous anger. Even the fight with Cal Runyon assumed sensible aspects, and he supposed that everything had been quite clear to Runyon; this would be a source of embarrassment now.

Leaving the hotel, the Kid walked in a roundabout way to Cadmus Rindo's large house and was admitted. Rindo was in his study and he looked around when the servant announced the sheriff.

The old man had his chair drawn up by the window where he could observe a portion of his town. Through the walls filtered the buzz and rip of the planing mill, and even here the pungency of the slab burner perfumed the air. "Sit down," Rindo said. He had been reading and now put his book aside. Very carefully he tamped tobacco into his pipe and lit it. "I've been wondering if you'd come."

"Any reason I shouldn't?" the Kid asked.

"You shot an innocent man," Rindo said. When the Kid opened his mouth to speak, Rindo held up his hand. "I know, you couldn't have done anything else, Pete being what he was. Rather fight than talk. I meant to fire him a dozen times, but never did. Some men just can't take care of themselves, and as long as he worked for me, I figured he wouldn't get into any serious trouble." He brushed his mustache. "Seems I was wrong."

"Another one of your misfits?"

Rindo's head came around quickly; then his expression softened. "You're learning fast, Kid. Yes, Pete was a down-and-outer. In one jail after another. He was pretty good with a gun, though, and took my orders until you came here."

"But you seem sure he didn't shoot Bess Jamison's man."

"Not positive, but I knew that wasn't Pete's way, Kid. He liked to face a man out. He did with you, didn't he? A man he must have known he couldn't beat."

"Yes," the Kid said bleakly. "He made it self-defense for me."

Rindo drew on his gurgling pipe. "Well, you didn't come here to tell me how sorry you feel for yourself. Got a suspect?"

"Any man who hates you," the Kid said.

"Ha!" Rindo slapped the arms of his chair. "Then go take your pick from the voting register."

The Kid considered this for a moment, then asked, "What does Ben Colfax have against you, Mr. Rindo?"

"Nothin' more than anyone else has," Rindo stated. "He's a perennial down-and-outer. Lots of them in this world. I pay no attention to how people feel about me. I understand it and I expect it. You're young, but someday you're going to find out that one good turn don't necessarily deserve another."

Gnawing his lip, the Kid turned several possibilities over in his mind. "Assuming that Pete was telling the truth, that he didn't kill the teamster, then we'll have to assume that Ben is lying. What does Ben stand to gain by telling something that won't hold up? Seems that the risks were pretty great."

"Hold on," Rindo said. "As long as you're figurin' that way, why not go back and figure Pete did do the shooting. He could have changed guns. He could own more than one, you know."

"That's a possibility I hadn't considered," the Kid said. "I'll have to check it." He picked up his hat, thanked Cadmus Rindo for the visit and started back toward his office.

When he passed the newspaper office, Nan Buckley hailed him and he stopped.

She handed him his revolver, holding it by the barrel. "You dropped this last night. I cleaned it good."

He slipped Ben Colfax' gun into his waistband, and his own into the holster. "Thanks," he said and started away, but her voice stopped him.

"Kid, do you hate me?"

"No."

"But you no longer believe in me. Is that it?"

"About it," he said. "Forget it, Nan. You don't owe me a thing."

"I don't believe that," she said. "We all owe something to someone."

He left her and walked slowly along the main street, wishing that he could hate her, for that would simplify everything. As the Kid approached the hotel porch, Wade Boomhauer stepped out. Too late to alter his course, the Wind River Kid stopped.

"Wonderful what a few hours' sleep will do for a man," Boomhauer said. He smiled and looked toward the planing mill as though trying to identify all the blending sounds of saw and planer. "A hell of a racket, ain't it?"

"Pretty noisy, but you get used to it."

"I may not be here that long," Boomhauer said. He patted his pockets a moment.

"Sheriff, do you have a cigar you could spare?" The Kid found a Moonshine Crook and offered it. "Thanks. A light? Yes, I can't seem to find matches either." He bent forward, cupping his hand around the flame.

The clatter and rush of horsemen at the head of the street caused both of them to straighten. Bess Jamison was running down in her buggy, while behind her, twenty mounted men made a tight wedge, driving all other traffic to the sides of the street.

She saw the Kid on the hotel porch and pulled up suddenly. The men sawed to a halt behind her and the Kid stepped to the street's edge. Bess Jamison did not bother to dismount. She had a double-barreled shotgun on the seat beside her, and she placed her hand on the stock, near the trigger guard. "We've come for the man who killed Allen. He was my driver."

"You're a little late," the Wind River Kid said evenly. "The man is dead. Killed resisting arrest."

Bess looked around, at the gathering crowd and at her own men. Then her attention swung back to the Kid. "I'm not going to call you a liar, but you're Rindo's law, and I find it hard to believe."

"I'm afraid you will have to believe it," Wade Boomhauer said evenly. "I happened

184

to be there too."

Bess turned toward him. "And who the devil are you?"

"Boomhauer, United States marshal," he said, making a slight bow from the hips.

Before Bess could say anything, the Kid slid his easy voice into the gap of silence. "There'll be an inquest in the morning. I'd advise you to be here for it." He took a step closer to the buggy. "And don't bring armed men into this town again."

"I've got a right to protect myself," Bess Jamison said.

"The law will do that for you," the Kid told her. He stepped back so she could turn the rig, but instead of that, she looked at Boomhauer.

"You after somebody?" she asked.

The Wind River Kid tensed, knowing that his moment had arrived. He tuned so that he faced Boomhauer. The marshal spoke around his cigar. "We have reason to believe that the Wind River Kid is in this vicinity."

"Reason?" Bess Jamison laughed. Here was, the Kid decided, her best opportunity to get rid of him without raising a hand. In her eyes he was Cadmus Rindo's law, bought and paid for, and because of that, her enemy. Few people could resist such an opportunity and the Kid held out no hope that Bess would pass this up. And she didn't. She pointed the stock of her buggy whip at him and said, "There's your Wind River Kid!" Her smile was triumphant. "Let's see you get out of this one, *sheriff.*" Lashing her team, she stormed down the street, her armed retinue following her.

She left a wake of silence. The spectators along the walk stood absolutely motionless. Wade Boomhauer took his cigar from his mouth and cast it into the street. "What about it, sheriff?"

"I'm the Wind River Kid. Can we talk about this, Wade?"

"Afraid not," Boomhauer said. "You know what I have to do."

"Just a minute," the Kid said. "Wade, I came into this town as nothing, but now it's changed. I got elected as a bad joke, but it's turned out to be more than that for me. Wade, I need this town and it needs me. You going to take that away from both of us?"

"Can't help it," Wade Boomhauer said. "It's my job, Kid."

"Then I'll have to fight you," the Kid said. "You give me no choice, Wade."

Boomhauer nodded. "Figured it would be that way," he said and drew.

He was good. His draw was clean and fast,

the product of long practice, and he was not a fancy gun-handler; he ignored hammer fanning, merely squeezing off when the muzzle flipped level.

But the Wind River Kid was palming up his own gun, the one lavishly tuned by a superior gunsmith. And that gun was in gifted hands. Although he gave Boomhauer the first move, he had him beat by the time the marshal slipped the barrel clear of the holster. No killing shot this time; the Kid put his bullet deliberately in Boomhauer's gun arm, fracturing it.

Boomhauer's bullet went a foot wide, since shock had started to spin him. His gun fell and he staggered back, fingers vising the torn flesh. He would have fallen had not a man stepped down and caught him. The Kid rushed forward, flung an arm around Boomhauer and helped him into the hotel lobby. To one of the bystanders he said, "Get Carver; don't just stand there!"

There was haste in his voice and anxiety, and regret for what he had done. He brushed others aside who tried to help, then tore at Boomhauer's sleeve, exposing the torn flesh and pumping blood. Boomhauer's complexion was chalky and shock made his eyes glisten. He spoke with an effort. "You could have — put that dead center —

instead of just in an arm."

"Why did you have to draw on me?" the Kid asked. "Hell, Wade, I didn't want to do this."

"Got a job to do," he said.

From the doorway came the doctor's shrill voice demanding to be let through. He knelt by the Kid and made his examination, then opened his satchel. "If ether makes you people sick, I'd advise you to leave." He handed the bottle and cone to the Kid. "Put that over his nose and add the ether a drop at a time." While the Kid followed directions, Dr. Carver continued his rough-mannered preparations. "Bullet just seems to have nicked the bone. Damned lucky it isn't a compound fracture. Splint? Where the hell did I put splints? You there, run into the kitchen and bring me some kindling." He looked at the Kid. "You do this?"

"Yes," the Kid said. "How much of this stuff do I pour on the cloth?"

Dr. Carver lifted one of Boomhauer's eyelids. "That's enough for awhile." He stood up and began flailing his arms at the crowd. "Get out! What do you think this is, a sideshow?"

They fell back before this shouting attack and when the lobby had been cleared, he came back and set Boomhauer's arm. While he was bandaging it, he said, "If he was after you, I wouldn't worry about it. He'll be a mighty sick man for a few days." He paused to cork the ether bottle. "Be a week before he feels like walking."

"Then I've bought myself a little time," the Kid said and went out.

There was a good-sized crowd still cluttering the boardwalk, but he pressed through and went on to the jail. When he opened the door, he found Ben Colfax sitting at the desk, his feet elevated. He dropped them quickly to the floor and said, "Been looking all over town for you." He got up when the Kid came around the desk.

"Not very damned hard," the Kid said. "What do you want, Ben?"

"If you're through with my gun, I'd like it back," he said.

The Wind River Kid slipped his own gun out of the holster and laid it on the desk. From his waistband he took Ben's gun, crammed it into the leather and handed the whole rig over. Without looking at Ben Colfax he said, "That story of yours about Pete shooting the teamster doesn't hold up. Pete was carrying the wrong caliber gun."

"Maybe he had another," Ben said. He tipped a chair against the wall and sat down. "Bein' a peace officer with years of experience, I'd say that Pete simply switched guns on you. Any good gunman's got a spare."

"You mean he threw the other one away?"

"Ain't likely," Ben said, smiling. "Pete's kind spends good money on their guns; he wouldn't throw one away. His horse around?"

"I think someone took it to the livery," the Kid said.

"Suppose we go take a look." He got up. "Don't mean to tell you your job, but you might as well take advantage of my experience."

The Wind River Kid had a refusal on the tip of his tongue, but he held it back. "All right," he said, "let's go take a look."

Darkness was only a matter of minutes away when they stepped outside, turning toward the stable at the end of the street. The building was dark except for the lamp glowing over the arch. They stopped just outside, both squinting, trying to cut the muddy gloom. Ben said, "You see if you can find a lantern. I'll try and locate Pete's horse."

He moved away before the Kid could say anything. By the time the Kid located and lighted a lantern, Ben was grumbling and stumbling around one of the rear stalls.

"Found him!" he called. "Come on back, Kid."

With a glow of light preceding him, the Kid walked toward the back of the building. Ben was in a box stall, his fingers fumbling with the lashings of Pete's bedroll and saddlebags.

"If it's here at all," Ben said, "it'll have to be in his blankets or bags. Put there before you shot him."

The Kid's glance came around; he was surprised at Colfax' cleverness, and made a point to remember that this man was smarter than he looked. "Let me have the blankets," he said.

But Ben was already spreading them out. "Take the bags," he said.

Ben was pawing the blankets apart while the Kid sounded the saddlebags. He found Pete's shaving gear, a spare pair of socks, then the gun. "Here's something," he said. "Bring the light around."

With the yellow flow of light over his shoulder, he read the caliber: .44 S & W American. Finding the gun made his case as complete as anyone could make it; he felt a vast relief, for his conscience had been riding him for having shot an innocent man, even in self-defense.

"He was Rindo's man," Ben Colfax said.

"The old man will have some explaining to do at the inquest."

"I'll need you there for a witness," the Wind River Kid said.

"Be obliged to tell what I know," Colfax said. He kicked Pete's belongings under the feed bin. "People around here know me, Kid. My testimony will give weight to the proceedings." He slapped the Kid on the arm and walked out, his shoulders bent, his head down as though he were studying tracks on the ground ahead of him.

Leaving the livery, the Kid decided to speak to Cadmus Rindo, for in his mind he felt that the old man should be told about Pete's guilt. Facing a coroner's inquest in the morning, Rindo would be at a terrible disadvantage if this proof were thrown unexpectedly in his face. Yet as he walked along the street, the Kid thought of that bullet collection Dr. Carver had. Could any of the other bullets there have been fired from a .44 American?

Dr. Carver was in his library, and he put his book aside when the Kid stepped in. "Sorry to interrupt," the Kid told him, "but I'd like to have another look at those bullets you saved."

"Certainly," Carver said, taking the lamp so he could go ahead to his laboratory. He placed the box of bullets on the table; each tagged and cushioned in cotton. "This one," he said, "was taken from Dale Pritchard, an attorney who was killed here about a year ago."

"How did it happen?" the Kid asked, taking the bullet and swinging around toward the lamp.

"No one knows," Carver admitted. "Knew the man pretty well too. Played cards with him regularly at Burkhauser's." He looked at the Kid and saw his sharpened expression. "Find something?"

"It's a .44 American," the Kid said. He laid the bullet down. "After Pritchard was shot, was that when the card games broke up for good?"

Carver looked a bit uneasy. "You know about that? How the devil —" Then he shrugged. "It's no matter really. Burkhauser, Ben Colfax, the judge, myself and Pritchard had a sort of private club." He paused as a man will when he wants a relatively bad thing to sound relatively good. "We were always hashing over some scheme to take control away from Rindo." He laughed hollowly. "It was really just a way to pass the time."

"Someone didn't think so," the Kid said. "Looks like Pete took his job seriously

193

enough to kill more than one man to keep it. Where was Pritchard shot?"

"Behind Burkhauser's place," Carver said. "The body was found near the gap between the buildings. Someone had been waiting for him."

"I thought that side door was a secret."

"Seems that it isn't, seeing as how you know about it," Carver said. "Ben Colfax investigated for weeks but couldn't turn up a thing." He sighed and wiped his mouth. "Makes me stop and think. Rindo must have known all the time; who else gave Pete his orders?"

"Let's see the bullet that killed Bess Jamison's father," the Kid said.

Carver fished through the tagged lead, then laid another in the sheriff's palm. "A .44 American?"

"Yes," the Kid said. "Can I have these three bullets?"

"That's evidence," Carver said. "Will you sign a paper for them?"

"Certainly," the Kid said and waited while Carver wrote out the description and circumstances pertaining to their removal. The Kid affixed his signature, then put the bullets into a small paper box that the doctor gave him. At the door he asked, "Is Boomhauer still at the hotel?"

"Yes," Carver said. "I intend to check on him later on."

Leaving the doctor's house, the Kid walked slowly toward the center of town. The matching bullets put Cadmus Rindo in a bad light. He knew only the barest rudiments of how business was run, but he was smart enough to know that the moment Rindo was indicted, Rindo's Springs would go to rack and ruin. The notes held by the merchants would be nearly worthless for Rindo could not pay off. The economy of the town would hit the bottom with such a whack that it might never recover.

As he passed the newspaper office, Nan Buckley spoke from the dark doorway. "Lost your last friend, Kid?"

He stopped and turned to her. "Nan," he said softly, "you told me once that you never wanted to see Rindo's Springs die. Well, I have to do what you didn't want done. I can't help myself, Nan."

"What are you talking about?" She stepped up to him and took his arm. "Kid, you've got to tell me."

"Come along," he said.

"All right." She drew a shawl around her shoulders and walked with him to the hotel. They met the clerk coming down the stairs, a tray full of dishes neatly balanced.

In passing, the Kid asked, "The marshal awake?"

"Yes," the clerk said. "Room six. We moved him to the second floor where there's a little more quiet."

The wall lamps puddled a dirty yellow light on the carpet. At the far end of the hall, the Kid opened the door without knocking, then stepped aside so that Nan could enter first. Boomhauer was propped up in bed. His face was gray although a strong dose of laudanum had deadened the major run of his pain. The Kid made a hurried introduction of Nan, then pushed two chairs close to the bed.

"I've got a nerve coming here like this," the Kid said, "but I need help. This job has kept me guessing; I don't know much about the law. All I can go by is what I think is right and wrong." He glanced at Nan, then launched into the history of Rindo's Springs, making clear the town's dependence on Cadmus Rindo. He described in detail the trouble Rindo had with Bess Jamison's father, and with the daughter after the father was shot. Without taking sides, the Kid laid out the rewards and consequences should anyone succeed in dethroning the old man. Then he produced the bullets, filling Boomhauer in on the details, and his suspicions. When he finished, he sat back in his chair, his young face grave.

"I would say," Boomhauer offered, "that you have a poor case against Cadmus Rindo." He put the bullets back in the box. "I have no doubt that a conviction is impossible; you have nothing to link him to the shootings. However, as you say, the town will collapse if you even let out a suspicion that he could have had anything to do with the deaths. Quite a problem. Throws the law books out the window and places everything on a man's conscience, doesn't it?"

"Yes," the Kid said softly. "Wade, some men in this town have been waiting for the day to come when they could make people believe that Rindo was through. Money is waiting to buy up Rindo's notes at ten cents on the dollar, and when that happens there won't be a town. People have to trust each other in order to do business. If I arrest Rindo, the trust will be wiped out. He's an anchor for everyone here. Now, what if I don't choose to sink the town just to get one man?"

Boomhauer's face was thoughtful. "You know the answer," he said. "As soon as I can walk, I'll take over and do the job for you." He let a small gap of silence build. "Kid, I've been in this business for eight years. It's what I wanted to be. You have no right to temper the law with your own feelings; if that happened often, there wouldn't be any law to turn to." He locked eyes with the Wind River Kid. "As soon as I'm able I'm going to arrest you, Kid. I'll come after you again. Maybe it won't be in the arm the next time, but as long as I carry this badge, I've got to try. And if I don't make it, I'll know that somewhere another badge will take up where I left off."

"What kind of man are you?" Nan asked flatly.

"He's a lawman," the Kid said, rising. "And a much better one than me." He opened the door for Nan Buckley and she stepped through. The Kid paused and said, "Wade, I like this town, so I'm going to play this the stupid way."

"I thought you would," Boomhauer said. "Good luck, Kid."

The Kid flashed him a grin and went down the hall with Nan Buckley. When they reached the boardwalk they stopped.

"Thanks for making the decision I wanted you to make," she said. She looked at him steadily, her eyes bright. "And yet in a way I'm sorry because you had to take sides. A compromise has always come hard for you, hasn't it? Perhaps that was what made me like you from the start."

She turned before he could speak and hurried down the street. He waited until she passed from sight around the corner, then stepped off the walk, angling toward Burkhauser's saloon.

9

Halfway across the street, the Wind River Kid stopped and retraced his steps. Reentering the hotel, he went to Will Beau-Haven's door and knocked, then waited with a growing impatience until Grace opened it. She seemed quite surprised to see him, but stepped aside and ushered him in. She wore an old pair of carpet slippers and they flapped loosely as she led the way to the gallery where Will Beau-Haven was taking his nightly observation of the town.

"The sheriff's here," she said and sat down. Lamplight dribbled through the open door and in this feeble light she resumed her interrupted knitting.

"Thought you'd be back," Beau-Haven said. He waited until the Kid pulled a chair around and sat down. "The town's getting nervous, I can feel it. People here are like a little kid who thinks his father's holding him down. The kid swears he'll up and leave home, but few do because they can't lose pa to lean on. The word's already around that you and Ben found the gun Pete used to kill the Jamison teamster. Pete worked for Rindo and Rindo was quarreling with Bess Jamison. Pretty obvious conclusion there, huh?"

"It's not proof," the Kid said. "No proof at all."

"True," Beau-Haven admitted, "but it's enough to start a run on Rindo's bank. You wait until it opens in the morning and you'll see the line." He turned to his wife. "Hand me that box of cigars there." Then he offered one to the Kid, and a light.

Between puffs, the Kid asked, "Who was Dale Pritchard?"

"So you found out about him?" Beau-Haven shrugged. "A smart lawyer. Too smart maybe."

"Part of the poker club?"

Beau-Haven chuckled. "Doc always did talk too much. Yes, Pritchard was as greedy as the rest. Came here as Rindo's lawyer. Quit him after a year or two and established a private practice. Talk has it that the judge, Ben Colfax and Murray Burkhauser financed him. No proof of it though." He paused to taste the fragrance of his cigar. "Whatever went on at those poker games is all over, sheriff. That door has been boarded up for months now." He turned his head and looked carefully at the young man. "What's so interesting about Pritchard? Most people have forgot about him by now."

"Any man whose death has never been explained is worth asking about," the Kid said. He got up. "Well, thanks for the cigar."

"I'll show you out," Grace Beau-Haven said tonelessly and laid her knitting aside. Her expression was as immobile as cement. The Kid followed her to the hall door.

She said a brief goodnight, then closed the door, listening to his footsteps recede down the hall. When she was positive that he had left the building, she walked back to the gallery.

"Time to come in now, Will."

"Ah, let me finish my cigar," he said.

"Now you can have another cigar tomorrow," she said. He grumbled something and she wheeled his chair toward the double doors. She placed him alongside his bed. With an effort she helped him shift his weight out of the chair. And when she leaned over to undress him, he took her arms and tried to pull her to him.

Her hands set up a gentle but firm resistance. "Please," she said, "you're just getting yourself worked up again."

His expression turned angry and desperate and packed with frustration. "Can I help wanting you with my mind, even though I can't do anything about it?"

She pulled away from him and fussed with his covers. "You have to stop thinking about it," she said. "Will, I've tried not to disturb you."

"Disturb me?" He looked at the ceiling and laughed. "Grace, do you think a sack dress can disguise what I already know?" He clenched his fists and struck his misshapen thighs, his mangled hips.

"I'll get you the tonic so you can sleep," she said and hurried from the room. When she came back, he was staring at the ceiling with dulled eyes. The tonic was downed without protest and he sagged back on his pillow. She turned the lamp down and went to the door. "You'll sleep now, Will. Please try."

"Where will you be?"

"Always near you," she said. "I bought a new book called *Ben Hur.* Perhaps you'd like to read —"

"No, no," he said, waving his hand. "God knows you have so little pleasure, Grace; I'd not deny you that."

"Goodnight, Will."

He did not answer her; he rarely did. She

closed the door softly and went into the parlor. The hanging wall clock ticked steadily on and she glanced at it: a quarter to nine. Early, she thought, and settled down with her book.

When the Kid stepped into Murray Burkhauser's saloon, heads turned, gave him a brief glance, then swung back to their own interests. He sagged against the bar, signaled for service, and the bartender edged up. "A tall beer," the Kid said. "Murray in the back?"

"No, he's playing cards over to Judge Richmond's house."

The Kid successfully masked his interest. "Oh, with Doc and Ben Colfax?"

"You got it right," the bartender said, moving away.

Toying with his beer, the Kid considered this for what it was worth. The door Beau-Haven said was no longer in use did not mean the end of the poker games, or the talk that must pass back and forth. The game went on and the Kid was certain that the stakes were not always on the table. But four-handed poker was a poor game; a fifth member made it more interesting. Dale Pritchard had been the fifth. Now the Kid wondered who had taken his place.

Finishing his beer, he went out and down the street. Traffic was light, a few horsemen and fewer pedestrians. At a quiet corner, the Kid ducked down a dark side street, walking slowly until he came to the alley behind the saloon. Dodging litter, he made careful progress until he came to the gap between the saloon and the store. To make sure he had the right place, he took a quick sight through and saw the upper gallery of the hotel. With half a mind he noticed that Will Beau-Haven was no longer at his post. Easing into the slot, the Kid found it free of debris. Normally such an opening would be a catch-all for stray whiskey bottles, but here everything had been carefully picked up. The night was ink here and he gently felt along the wall of the saloon until he found the boarded-up section. All along the Kid had felt that he was onto something important here, but now he felt a keen disappointment.

Still, he made a careful examination with his hands, and oddly enough, found that all the boards were cut to exactly the same length. This struck an off-key chord in his mind, for he knew how haphazardly a place was usually closed up — a carpenter did not bother with exact measurements and cuts.

Yet this was a good job, tight-fitting and perfectly laid out. Returning to the alley, the Kid found a tin-can lid, then returned to the section of the wall and carefully tested the ends of the sawed boards. The lid went in deep, clearly outlining a doorway.

Satisfied now, the Kid found a piece of paper and wedged it carefully into the crack. Tomorrow he would come back and look for it. If it was still there, he would know that the door had remained closed. If it had fallen, then he'd have to lay plans to find out who used the door.

Leaving the alley, he walked down the quiet street toward Cadmus Rindo's house. There was a light on in the old man's study and the Kid knocked. A moment later the servant admitted him. Rindo was sitting by a small table, reading. He put the book down and waved the Kid into a chair. "Sort of been expecting you," he said. "I hear tell you found Pete's other gun."

"Yes," the Kid said flatly. He took a chance and added, "That same gun killed Bess Jamison's father and Dale Pritchard. Do you know what that adds up to?"

"That I ordered it done," Rindo said. He waved his hand. "Don't matter. I'd be accused of it anyway."

"Some people will say that it's proof

enough."

The old man's eyes squinted. "What do you say?"

"It doesn't make much sense," the Kid said. "Hell, of all people you know best what'll happen here if there's open trouble. Shooting Bess's old man was a sure way to start it. So was killing the teamster. Unless you're trying to put yourself under, you'd have no reason to have 'em killed."

"That's my whole point," Rindo said. "No matter how Ben or any of the others twist it, I'd gain the least by starting trouble." He smiled. "Being as you're a man who's seen his share of trouble, I was counting on you to see it." His humor vanished. "How does it look up town, Kid?"

"Not good," the Kid admitted. "Beau-Haven thinks there'll be a run on the bank in the morning."

"I'd better call Cal Runyon," Rindo said and rang a small bell to summon his servant. When the man appeared, Rindo said, "Go to the company office and fetch Cal Runyon here."

The servant turned to go, then faced around again. "Beggin' pahdon, suh, but Mistah Runyon's ovah to the judge's house playin' pokah. This is Thursday, suh."

"Go get him anyway," Rindo said, sagging

back as the servant went out.

The Kid was relieved when Rindo clung to a brief silence, for he was trying to fit Runyon into the poker club, to attach some meaning for this small but very select group. Somehow, in his mind, this group had become synonymous with Cadmus Rindo's troubles.

He looked up suddenly and found the old man's sharp eyes reading him. Rindo said, "You play poker, Kid?"

"Probably not the way Runyon plays," the Kid said. He leaned forward, his curiosity out of control. "Old man, don't you care?"

Rindo started to chuckle. "Kid, if I jumped every time a rabbit rustled in the brush, I'd be jumpin' all the time. Cal Runyon's a human being. And don't you forget it." He leaned back in his chair and folded his gnarled hands in his lap. "For nigh onto forty years now, I've put up with this sort of thing. Sure, I could ride herd on these folks, but there's no need to. Give 'em their chance to talk and plan and scheme and get frustrated. As long as I'm alive, there's nothing they can really do."

"They can kill you," the Kid said.

"That's likely," Rindo said. "But who's goin' to do it? Ben Colfax? Naw! Ben don't want to get hung while everyone licks up the gravy. Oh, Ben'd like to see me dead, but he wouldn't do it."

"What about Burkhauser and the judge and Doc Carver?"

"Same thing," Rindo said. "They've been talkin' about it for a long time, but they still haven't settled that one important detail: who's going to pull the trigger." He sighed and packed his pipe. "Son, you're settin' there, mind a-churnin' away, trying to figure out who killed who. It does bother me, the way you always keep lookin' for a man's dark side. Why should you look for something we all know is there? Look toward his good, son. Life's a lot more pleasant that way."

"I can't make up my mind," the Kid said, "whether you're a great man or a damn fool."

"A blend," Rindo said. "Just like all other men." He turned his head when steps crossed the porch. "That'll be Cal." He got up and poured a drink and had it waiting when the young general superintendent came in. Runyon nodded to the Kid and picked up the glass. Rindo asked, "How was the game?"

"Dull," Runyon admitted. He checked his watch. "I hope this won't take too long. I'm thirty-seven dollars in the hole, and I'd like to make it back before midnight."

"Maybe I can add a little fresh blood," the Kid suggested gently.

"I'd like that," Runyon said. He drank his whiskey and looked at Cadmus Rindo.

The old man said, "Before the bank opens in the morning, take that eighteen thousand that's in the company safe and transfer it to the bank's vault. The Kid here heard a rumor of a run."

The Wind River Kid stared, for this was not what he had expected. When he opened his mouth to protest, Rindo smiled and shushed him with a wave of his hand. "Son, when there's going to be a run on a bank, there's nothing like money to stop it. If a depositor's scared, his philosophy is: if you have it, I don't want it, and if you haven't got it, I want it now." His glance touched Runyon. "See that the money gets there." He pushed himself erect. "Bedtime, gents. And, both of you, stop stewin' and get a decent night's sleep."

Cal Runyon and the Kid left the house together, taking another back street toward the judge's place. Runyon walked in silence for a time, then said, "He's a great old man, Kid. I'd like to see him outlive all of us."

"He may at that," the Kid said.

The shades were pulled in the judge's

parlor, but fragments of light squeezed through at the bottom. Runyon went in without knocking and they looked around, surprised to see the Kid with him. Burkhauser pulled up a chair and said, "I hope you've got cash. My luck's terrible and some new money will look good."

Judge Richmond nodded and Carver peered over his glasses. Ben Colfax mumbled a greeting, then put his attention on the shuffle. "Stud," he said. "A dollar ante."

He flipped the cards with a certain clumsiness, one to each man, all face up except his own. The Kid had a queen showing so he bet another dollar. "That-a-boy!" Burkhauser said. "Go slow here. Remember the poor working man."

Again Ben Colfax put out a round of cards, face up. Runyon drew a ten to match the one he got on the first round. Ben Colfax peeked at his hole card, then said, "Make up your mind, Cal."

"I'll go two," he said and slid his money onto the table. Richmond licked his lips and looked at the five and six he had; he seemed to have difficulty deciding whether to stay in or drop out. But he was a long-shot player at heart and put in his money.

Again the cards went around. "There's

whiskey if you want it," Burkhauser said. No one seemed to care for a drink. Burkhauser was moodily studying his cards while Ben Colfax contemplated two jacks. The Kid had a queen and a pair of nines.

"Jacks bet," Colfax said, "ten dollars."

Richmond threw in his hand and the Kid could not help thinking how right Rindo was: the judge for one did not have the courage to kill a man. Murray Burkhauser made a great fuss over his cards, but he was too conservative to take chances; his went into the discards. Runyon played it out, as did Carver and the Kid, only Carver was lost before he started. He was a man who tried to reduce the game to scientific principles, ignoring the strong character of the players.

When all cards were out, Runyon and Carver gave up, after contributing thirty-five dollars apiece to the pot. The Kid looked at Ben Colfax crouching over his cards. Colfax had his pair of jacks and an ace showing, against the Kid's pair of nines and the solitary queen. "Jacks, ace bet," the Kid said.

Ben took his time, making the wait tedious even for those already dropped out. He did not look more than once at his hole card, implying that it was so good as to become unforgettable. His flat glance touched the Kid, then he said, "How much you got there?" indicating the coins by the Kid's elbow.

"About a hundred dollars."

"That's my bet," Colfax said, thrusting that amount to the center of the table.

The Wind River Kid began to dig into his pockets and came up with some bills. He added this to the gold, then said, "Raise you seventy-five."

A muscle twitched in Ben Colfax' cheek and his eyes pulled together slightly. Murray Burkhauser said, "Put up or shut up, Ben. You've been tapping us all night."

The Kid waited; then with a growl of disgust Ben threw in his hand. His hole card was a deuce of spades. Scooping the money toward him, the Kid counted it, put most of it away, then took the deal. "Five-card draw," he said, "since it's dealer's choice."

He played for an hour and a half, winning some, losing some, but generally winning from the judge and Cal Runyon. Carver's mathematics were confounding, for the man played a straight game, so straight that it was confusing. Carver was a sure-thing player and the moment he suspected that the cards were falling wrong, he dropped out.

Burkhauser had been a professional too long to play for anyone but the house. He possessed no individual daring, especially when betting his own money.

The real study was Ben Colfax, and the Kid bent all his mental faculties trying to keep abreast of the man. Twice Colfax drew to an inside straight and made it. Given the slightest chance, Ben Colfax would either make his cards or bluff the others into submission.

At a quarter to twelve, Murray Burkhauser yawned and slid back his chair. "Closing time," he said. "I've got to see if the bartender made back what I've lost."

He got into his coat and said goodnight. The Kid glanced at his watch while Cal Runyon said, "Hey now, big winners don't walk out so easy."

"I can spare an hour or two," the Kid admitted.

"An hour for me," Colfax said. "Way past my roosting time." He looked around the table. "Who's got the deal? Doc? Let's get 'em out then." He spun a dollar onto the table and leaned back, smiling at the Wind River Kid.

When the wall clock struck eleven, Grace Beau-Haven put down *Ben Hur* and went into her bedroom. There she kindled a small fire and heated water for her bath. She undressed and stood before a full length mirror, studying herself. Shed of the drab and shapeless dress, she was a woman alive and beautiful, with a body delightfully burned in flawless curves. Her breasts were high and firm, her hips boyishly trim and her muscles as smooth as a runner's.

Impatient with the heating water she dumped it lukewarm into a large pewter tub then lowered herself into it. Her bath was leisurely and after blotting herself dry, she sprayed her neck and shoulders with cologne. Afterward she re-hid the bottle on the top closet shelf.

From a hidden alcove she took out a dress that was pale blue and as light as a cloud. She shook it just to hear the silk rustle, then giggled, so profound was her pleasure.

Donning fragile silk underclothes and lace-trimmed petticoats, she moved gracefully about, humming in an almost breathless way. Finally she slipped into the dress, fought the row of tiny buttons up the back, then put on a pair of light shoes.

The clock had struck the half-hour some time before and she turned the lamps down before opening the hall door. No one was in sight and she moved toward the back entrance, which was always kept locked at night. Inserting a key, she let herself out, then relocked the door. A flight of steps let her down to the mud-black alley. She took the stairs carefully, yet rapidly, for she had a long-standing familiarity with them. Moving swiftly down the alley, she avoided noisy traps of litter, then stopped at the first cross street. All the business houses were closed and no one occupied the boardwalks. Quickly and unseen, she crossed to the other side, and halfway down, entered the alley.

Only by conscious effort did she keep herself from running, and with each step her impatience increased until it became almost unbearable. At a gap between the buildings she paused, but only for a second. Then she turned sideways and began to edge through. At the boarded door in Burkhauser's wall she scraped twice with her fingernails, then listened to his approaching step on the other side.

10

As was his long-established habit, Murray Burkhauser closed his saloon at eight minutes to twelve on Thursday nights. He took the cash from the bartender's box and carried it to his office. A turned key closed him off from the rest of Rindo's Springs and after putting the cash away, he ignited a cigar and waited.

Frequent glances at his watch kept him informed of the exact time, and when he heard two faint scratches on the wall, he lifted a metal wastebasket and placed it over the desk lamp. With the room smothered in darkness, Burkhauser stepped to the bookcase, pulled it from the wall so that Grace Beau-Haven could enter, then closed it quickly.

He then removed the metal basket from the lamp before the odor of heated metal grew thick in the room. With only the single light pushing at the darkness, they put their arms around each other and stood that way for many minutes, their lips locked, all else forgotten save their own driving passion. There was a touch of obscenity in the way Murray Burkhauser loved this woman: his hands pulled at the rounded flesh as though trying to devour it. His kiss indicated a passion starved beyond control, and he breathed heavily through his nose like a wrestler struggling to free himself from an inescapable grip. His animal hungers overwhelmed her until she merely submitted to his anxious hands, probing, caressing, fondling. There was no balance to his ardor, no scheme or semblance of order to his passion-mad thoughts. He would break off from a kiss to bite her on the neck, then abandon that to grind her body against his; he was a demented bee running amok in a flower garden, overwhelmed, unable to steady himself for a moment to drink from a single blossom. There was little satisfaction to this love; perhaps that drove him so furiously. His mind was riveted to only one thought finally and he pressed her back until she rested on his leather couch.

Grace Beau-Haven's hands pushed at him, trying to check his headlong rush, but he was beyond restraint. As before, she gave up and tried instead to match his insanity.

The wall clock ticked loudly and Burkhauser's breathing was a deep whistling as his lips sought the hollow of her throat. She knew this man and what he expected, so she moaned a little and bit him on the ear.

This seemed to be a sort of signal for he got up hurriedly and turned down the lamp until the room was thick with shadows. Her dress rustled as she stood up and Murray Burkhauser tore impatiently at the buttons on his vest and shirt.

"Hurry," she said softly, and this drove him to a frenzy of haste.

At four o'clock Murray Burkhauser got up and searched out a cigar. He padded about, naked and bare foot, the strong odor of sour sweat heavy in his nostrils. Fumbling about on his desk, his fingers contacted a cigar and he hastily put a match to it. In the glare he looked down at his body and felt a strong revulsion. Whipping out the match, he slipped quickly into pants and shirt.

This too seemed to be a signal, for near the shadows by the bed, Grace sat up, then began to shrug into her petticoats. Murray Burkhauser turned up the lamp and let the new light fling harsh shadows across his face.

"What time is it?" she asked.

He walked over to the wall clock and

peered at it. "Quarter past four." He stood there puffing on his cigar. His upper body was thick and roped with muscle and dark tufts of hair peeked through the open front of his shirt. "Are you all right?" he asked.

"Yes, I'm fine." He helped her fasten the back of her dress, then stood there watching her as she put on her shoes. He wondered if he had hurt her; sometimes he did, forgetting his strength, bruising her; once his fingernails had drawn blood.

"Do you want me to go with you?" he asked softly.

"No. Someone might see you."

Suddenly she put her elbows on her knees and looked at him. "Do you know how deep hell is, Murray?"

"What kind of crazy talk is that?" he asked. "Grace, you're not going to have one of your spells, are you?"

"No," she said. "I won't embarrass you, Murray. I know what appearances mean to you."

"Grace —"

"Don't start lying to me," she said quickly. "Don't start telling me that you want to marry me, because I know you don't. I merely serve a purpose in your life, Murray, and if I didn't, some other woman would."

"That's not true!"

"It's true," she said. "Murray, we just don't care about anyone but ourselves. We'll never do the right thing, because the right thing just isn't in us. Down to hell, that's where we're going." She giggled and this frightened him slightly, for her balance was precarious at best. "I don't know why I keep coming here, but I suppose it's because I need you. I don't love you when I leave. Just hate you because you always prove to me what I really am." She gathered the remainder of her things and went to the bookcase. He didn't want to argue with her; his only emotion now was one of impatience; he wanted to be left alone. She stepped down to ground level. They did not speak; goodbye was a needless word. Swiftly and silently she moved down the narrow gap.

Rindo's Springs was asleep; still she used caution navigating her way back to the rear entrance of the hotel. She was an expert at stealth, having practiced it for so long. Unlocking the door, she glanced down the hall, saw no one, then went quickly into her own rooms. The lamp still burned and she began to put her clothes away carefully.

Then she opened the connecting door that led into Will Beau-Haven's room. The side lamp by his bed was flickering, nearly out of kerosene, so she refilled it from a two-gallon can kept in the closet.

Will Beau-Haven lay on his back, his features immobile. For several minutes Grace stood there, looking at this man she had married. Then she reached out and touched his cheek and felt the waxy coldness there. Her eyes regarded him quite calmly, then she said, "I'll get you another blanket, dear."

When she tried to tuck the quilt about him, he felt strangely unyielding. A trembling started in her legs and worked through her until she shivered uncontrollably. She lay down beside him, her hand stroking his cold, bloodless cheek.

The sun woke her and she stared at the reflection cast on the ceiling by water in the washbasin. She felt very cold and when she got up her body ached and each movement was painful. Then she staggered into the other room, her eyes immobile in a stiff-set face. Carefully she dressed in the drab, ill-fitting dress, fixed her hair in its severe fashion, then powdered her face until her complexion was chalky. "I'm very modest," she said aloud. "A woman has to watch her appearance, men being what they are. But I really prefer gray; it's my best color."

Suddenly she went to the closet and took

out the lovely, hidden dresses. Carrying them to the heating stove, she stuffed them inside. A rolled paper and a match sent them roaring up in smoke while she stood there with a rapt expression, smiling and watching the hungry, bright flames.

When the fire died to a gray ash, she walked to the hall door and stood there, a drab, pathetic figure. The clerk was bustling about his duties in the lobby and he looked up, smiling when he saw her. "Good morning, Mrs. Beau-Haven."

Her expression was curiously wooden but her voice was quite deep. "Please send up breakfast for two."

The clerk nodded and she went back into her room. Standing by Will Beau-Haven's bed, she idly brushed his hair. "The sun's out this morning; you'll feel better when you get warm."

Finally the clerk came in with the tray. "Just set it there on the table," she said. "Will you help me get him into his chair, Joe?"

"Sure," the clerk said and followed her to Beau-Haven's bed. He looked at Beau-Haven, his eyes growing larger and rounder. Then he gave Grace a startled glance. "Mrs. Beau-Haven, he's — dead!"

"No, he's just chilled," she said softly.

"He'll feel better when he gets in the sun, Joe."

Like all sane people confronted with madness, the clerk regarded her with a tinge of fear. Slowly he backed toward the hall door, then made a dash for the stairs, yelling in a quavering voice.

11

Shortly after daybreak, the Kid left his lumpy cot in the sheriff's office and took a walk around town. A swamper was plying his broom on Burkhauser's porch, and down the street the butcher was opening his shop. After cruising both sides, the Kid eased into the alley behind the saloon, then into the gap between Burkhauser's and the store. He found his piece of paper on the ground and picked it up, a thin smile on his face. Quite understandable now was Burkhauser's pointed departure from the poker game.

Leaving the alley, the Kid walked to the restaurant and there had a heavy breakfast. By seven o'clock, a good crowd was developing on both sides of the street. Waiting for the bank to open, he decided, and ordered another cup of coffee.

Nan Buckley came down the street, looked in the window, then came in when she saw him at the counter. "I stopped at your office and you weren't there," she said. The waiter looked at her and she added, "A cup for me, Wong." Her fingers fastened in the Kid's sleeve. "What can we do about this?"

He shrugged. "Nothing. Did Bess Jamison come into town yet?"

"I haven't seen her. Besides, I don't give a damn about her. But there can't be enough money in the bank to pay off the depositors."

"Keep your voice down," he said, and finished his coffee. He swung around so that he faced her. "Why don't you just sit still and see what happens." A quick consultation with his watch told him that time was advancing. "I have an inquest to attend."

"You're awfully calm," she said half-accusingly, as though she envied him this display of unconcern.

The Kid left the restaurant. Pausing on the boardwalk, he looked at the crowd growing near the bank. Mostly small depositors, he judged; very few businessmen were there. This gave him some heart, for if Rindo could stand the strain of paying off for two hours, the word would get around that he had the money. And as he had said, if he had it, they soon wouldn't want it.

Returning to his office, he found Dr. Carver there. The little man's usually grave expression was even more cloudy and he kept drumming his fingers against the edge of the desk.

"Too much poker?" the Kid asked.

"Agh," Carver said. "I've been waiting for you." He took a sheaf of papers from an inner coat pocket. "Here's the report on Pete. You'll need it for the inquest."

"Thanks," the Kid said. He nodded toward the crowd around the bank. "If you have anything in there, you'd better get it out."

"There are other things to worry about," Carver said. He started toward the door, then stopped. "I don't suppose you heard, but Will Beau-Haven took too much medicine last night. On purpose. I found the empty bottle by his bed this morning."

"Dead?"

"Very. Happened around midnight, I'd say." He shrugged his thin shoulders. "He was a sick man anyway. It's his wife I feel sorry for. She found him and it must have snapped her reason. Hopelessly insane, I'm afraid."

He went out in the bustling way he had, as though there were a thousand things he had to do immediately. The Kid sat down on the corner of his desk, his eyes thoughtful.

Then on impulse he picked up his hat, left the office and walked along the main street until he came to Burkhauser's saloon. As he drew near, he became aware of hammering somewhere in back and a strange excitement charged through him. He felt as though he were nearing the end of something important.

The bartender was alone, bent below the counter rearranging his beer kegs. The Kid hurried through and went into the back where Murray kept his rooms. Burkhauser's door was open and the Kid stepped inside. The hammering was coming from the other side of the bookcase. He looked around, seeing the fine furniture, the ornate drapes and desk. Then he walked over to the bookcase and by feeling the vibration, located the door. A tug opened it and he smiled into Burkhauser's startled face.

"Doing a little carpenter work, Murray?"

A moment passed before Burkhauser spoke. "Wait there," he said. "I'm coming in."

"Good," the Kid said and shoved the bookcase closed again. He heard the rear door slam, then Burkhauser's step in the hall. When he came in, he slammed the door and threw the hammer in the corner.

Murray's expression said that he wanted to know how the Kid had caught on. The young man smiled and said, "Will Beau-Haven told me about it."

"That snoop!"

"Dead snoop," the Kid corrected. "It's peculiar how a man reaches conclusions. It all started with the poker club, before Dale Pritchard was killed. Beau-Haven said the door hadn't been used, yet the gap was kept clean. That struck me as odd, Murray. In my work the odd things can save your life." He patted his pockets for a cigar and when he failed to find one, took one of Burkhauser's. "Last night I stuck a piece of paper in the crack of that door and this morning found it on the ground. It fell there when the door was opened."

"Damned smart," Murray Burkhauser rumbled.

"You haven't heard the real smart part yet," the Kid said. "I kept asking myself why a man would leave an old group like your poker party to keep a midnight appointment. The answer was obvious." He smiled. "A woman, Murray. The answer had to be a woman." He shrugged and slapped his thighs. "You know, that discouraged me. It really did. All the time I hoped I was uncovering the group of men who were plotting to take Rindo's hair, and then it turned out that the door was for a woman. Real discouraging."

Murray Burkhauser stared, his mouth a fleshy O. "Plotting against — Jesus, we want to save this town!"

"Now that sounds pretty thin, Murray. But no mind now. When doc told me that Beau-Haven committed suicide in the night, and that his wife was out of her mind, I got a hunch. Ever have a hunch? No, I can see that you're a percentage player. So I came here, and sure enough, you were boarding the door up, which meant that it wouldn't be used again. Why? Because Grace Beau-Haven could never use it again."

The Kid had laid enough ammunition into the black to recognize a score when he made it; Burkhauser's bluff ran out, leaving him full of trouble. "You got a few things twisted," Murray said, pouring himself a glass of whiskey. He drank, then stood deep in thought for a moment. "I guess I know which side you're on, Kid. The town's side. And believe me, that's the only one that matters a damn to me." He looked suspiciously at the Kid. "Must sound bad, coming from me. I've lied and cheated all my life, and told myself that I wasn't really that way at all. But that was a lie too. Funny thing about a weak man. He can't stand without help. That's why Pritchard, Carver, Richmond, Colfax and me formed a little club. Bess Jamison's old man was raising hell; we could see a split-down-the-middle fight coming, and had an idea what it would do to the town. So we got set up for it, pooling money, intending to buy up enough to save Cadmus Rindo when he got forced to the wall."

"But Pritchard got killed," the Kid reminded him. "You waited a long time before taking in another man."

"We had to be sure! Hell, it couldn't be just anybody!" He wiped a hand across his mouth. "That run on the bank won't work, Kid. It won't work because a bunch of us deposited another thirteen thousand dollars this morning before it opened." He laughed with pride and he stood a little straighter. "Rindo can keep paying all day and never run dry. When people see that, they'll stop asking for their money."

This was a possibility that the Kid had completely ignored, that men could be trying to save the town as well as grab what they could for themselves. "Is this straight, Murray?"

"It's straight," he said. "But you can't say

anything about it."

"No, I can see that." He looked squarely at Burkhauser. "Now we come to the door."

"I made it," he said. "We had to have a place to meet that wasn't public. After Pritchard got shot, we figured that someone was on to us, so we never used it again." His glance was guilt-filled. "Then I got better acquainted with Grace. It was a rotten thing from the beginning, but I couldn't stop it. I don't think I wanted to stop it."

"Well, it's been stopped now," the Kid said. "Murray, do you think one of Rindo's men killed Pritchard?"

"Hell no! I heard about you matching bullets, but there's something wrong there, Kid. Pete wasn't a back-shooter for anyone, certainly not Cadmus Rindo. A gunman yes, but not an alley artist. He was proud of the fact that he faced his men."

The Kid glanced at his watch. "The inquest is going to begin in a few minutes." He got up and stepped to the door. "Thanks, Murray. Now I don't feel so alone."

"Wait! Kid, you don't owe this town anything. Why are you fighting for it?"

"Maybe for the same reason you are," he said. "I get a feeling here that I'm really better than I think I am. A good feeling,

Murray. Hate to lose it."

He grinned. "People ain't so bad, Kid. Even when they're sonsabitches."

"You're right," the Kid said and left.

The crowd at the bank was a noisy one, now that the doors were open and the cashiers were paying out as fast as they could count it. The sight of people emerging, counting their money, had a healthy effect on those trying to get in. Snatches of talk reached the Kid; one man standing near the crowd proclaimed in a loud voice, "Hell, they got it stacked up a foot high in there! More gold and paper than you ever seen before!"

Using these signs as a basis for judgment, the Kid suspected that the run was due for a short life. With this thought he turned and walked toward Judge Richmond's house.

A block away he could see that the clans had gathered; Cadmus Rindo's expensive buggy was parked by the white picket fence, as was Bess Jamison's mud-spattered rig. Surrounding these were the saddle horses belonging to Bess' men. They were standing in a tight group, stern-faced and silent. As the Kid walked by, they gave him blunt stares, but he could see that they had taken his earlier warning to heart; their weapons were in saddle scabbards.

Ben Colfax and Cal Runyon were standing on the judge's porch, talking, and when the Kid walked up the path, they broke this conversation off.

"Damned sad about Beau-Haven," Runyon said. "He worked for Rindo before I came here."

"Tough on his missus," Colfax murmured. "Doin's about ready to start, Kid."

They went into the judge's parlor and found the warring factions seated on opposite sides of the room. Bess Jamison stared at the Kid, her expression hostile. She and Cadmus Rindo, he decided, did not actually hate each other, but they had passed so many acid remarks back and forth that neither was willing to take anything back for fear of appearing weak. The Kid took a chair near Dr. Carver, and Judge Richmond rapped for order.

The proceedings went along smoothly, if not a bit dryly. Ben Colfax gave his testimony, and the Kid had to back him up with the physical evidence: the bullet taken from the teamster's body, and the matching gun that had been found in Pete's saddlebag.

Twice Bess Jamison got to her feet and started to protest, but Judge Richmond tolerated no nonsense, and she lapsed into an angry silence. There was only one verdict possible under the circumstances: the team-ster had been shot and killed by Pete Davis as a result of a quarrel that had taken place earlier. This seemed to outrage Bess, but Richmond moved on to the next business at hand, the shooting of Pete while resisting arrest.

This was a simple matter and was dis-pensed with in short order. Dr. Carver spoke up. "I have the extracted bullet, judge. Do you want to enter it as evidence?"

"I think not," Richmond said. "Mr. Run-yon was a witness to the affair." He rapped with his gavel and brought the inquest to a close.

Doc Carver nudged the Kid and dropped the bullet into his hand. "Keep it as a souvenir."

"I don't want the damn thing," the Kid said, but Carver was already moving away to talk to someone else.

Bess Jamison was one of the first to stalk out, followed by Ben Colfax. While Runyon edged over to speak to the Kid, Colfax took Bess by the arm and steered her to the edge of the porch. They talked for a moment, then walked down the path together, stop-ping near her buggy.

She gave Colfax a weary smile and said, "Damn little satisfaction I got out of that,

Ben. A man killed on each side."

"I know, I know," he said. "The sheriff is quite a fella. Gets his teeth right into a thing." He took off his hat and glanced at the sky. "Cloudin' up. Rain before nightfall." He replaced his hat and looked toward the porch. "Notice how close the Kid stays to Cal Runyon and Cadmus Rindo? Guess I don't have to tell you where the gods are sleepin'."

"Figured it would be that way when Rindo bought the election." She glanced at her men still standing idly by. "Don't run off, Charlie, Hank. The old boar's got to come out of his nest sometime."

"Wait now," Colfax said. "This ain't the place to start trouble. The Kid will stop it."

"Just let him try," Bess said. "We'll walk all over him."

Cadmus Rindo chose that time to come out of the house. He saw Bess and her men gathered by the gate, but came down the path as though he had it all to himself. His steps were slow and measured, the only concession he had made to his advanced years. At the gate he glanced her way, then turned his back on her and walked to his buggy.

This manner of aloofness offended Bess Jamison. "Old man!" she said sharply.

He pivoted slowly and gave her a calm stare. "Were you speaking to me?"

"You know damn well who I'm speaking to," she said. Detaching herself from her friends, she came over Rindo. "I guess you could afford to lose Pete Davis, but I couldn't spare my man. So I hardly call it a fair trade."

His voice held a hint of anger. "You speak of dead men as though they were dollars and cents passed back and forth." In disgust he turned from her, but she took his shoulder and spun him around again.

The Kid raised his head in time to see this storm brewing; he started down the path with rapid strides. Cadmus Rindo was saying, "Don't ever put hands on me again, woman!"

"This is what I think of your threats!" Bess whipped her hand across the old man's face, driving him back against the front wheel. The Kid had the gate open and was passing through when one of Bess's men, thinking to do her a favor, tried to stop him. The Kid sledged the man along the shelf of the jaw, spinning him into his stunned friends. Before anyone could stop him, he yanked Bess by the hair, then stood between her and Cadmus Rindo.

When she made the mistake of trying to

strike the Kid, he shoved her with the flat of his hand so hard that she nearly fell. "Get out of town and cool off," he said.

"You're not running me out! Rindo's paid flunky, that's all you are!"

"I told you to get!"

Cadmus Rindo's anger was in full bloom now and there was this insult to balance before Bess Jamison left town. He tried to push the Kid aside, and when he couldn't, walked around him, shaking his fist at Bess. "By thunder, you got me riled now! I put up with your pa and I've put up with you, but danged if I will any longer! You git, and don't come back! If you ain't off that property in twenty-four hours, I'll drive you off!"

"You just come ahead!" she yelled. "You'll get more'n you can handle!"

"Shut up, both of you!" the Kid snapped.

"Huh?" The idea alone was a shock to Cadmus Rindo. For a moment he thought he had heard incorrectly, but he hadn't; the Kid had told him to shut his mouth. And he had the nerve to repeat it.

"I said shut your fool mouth." He ignored the old man, facing Bess Jamison. "Now get out of town before you raise a fuss you can't get out of. Take your friends too."

"I'll go when I get danged good and

ready! You want to try to throw me out?"

"You'll cool off better in jail," he said and grabbed her arm before she could break away. Her men made a start for their horses and weapons, but Cal Runyon drew his .38 and said, "I wouldn't interfere with the law if I were you fellas." His voice was soft but the warning was sincere. They remained rooted.

Cadmus Rindo began to cackle and dance a jig; his patent leather shoes raised a tawny cloud of dust. "That's the kind of law I like," he yelled. "No fuss or feathers to it." He shook his fist at Bess Jamison. "Got your come-uppance, didn't you? Remember what I said, twenty-four hours!"

"Another word out of you," the Kid said, "and you can share the cell block with her."

"Huh?" Rindo said, his offense renewed. "You go plumb to hell! I do as I please."

The Kid hooked his fingers in the old man's coat and pulled him against Bess Jamison. Then he shoved both of them ahead of him, his arms stiffened. Cal Runyon brought up the rear, a heavy frown on his face, while Bess' entourage tagged along with Ben Colfax.

Had the Kid stopped shoving for an instant, he would have found his prisoners uncontrollable, but he kept them off balance and fighting each other more than they fought him. A spectacle like this drew a crowd; this was more exciting than a run on a bank. The danger there had dwindled to nothing, but the Kid wondered if he hadn't created a new and more deadly crisis.

Cadmus Rindo was being led to jail like a miscreant drunk and the Kid pondered the effect it would have on the citizens of the town. Most of them were laughing and cat-calling; there is nothing more comical to peasants than when their king loses his seat and falls from his great white horse.

At the jail a thoughtful citizen threw the door open and the Kid's shove propelled them both into the center of the room. The Kid whirled and locked the door while Ben Colfax began to pound on it.

"Let me in, Kid! Damn it, open up in there!"

Ignoring him, the Kid motioned toward the cell blocks down the hall. "All right, let's not waste any time about it now."

"Think you're smart, don't you?" Bess turned to Cadmus Rindo and glared for a moment, then her anger vanished, leaving her face strangely pleasant, just a pretty girl who found continuous anger a trial. "Well, as long as we're in the same boat, I can't say that there was favoritism, can I?"

She entered the cell meekly enough and allowed the Kid to lock the door. But when he tried to lock the door on Rindo, the old man became slightly panic-stricken. "Say now, this has gone far enough! By God, this is my town! My jail!"

"Then you hadn't ought to mind spending a little time in it," the Kid said, turning the key in the door. He went back to his office and let Ben Colfax in. Colfax looked grave around the mouth and kept stroking his mustache with his forefinger.

"Damn," he said, "but I never thought you'd lock up the old man."

"Don't we have a law here about disturbing the peace?"

"Yeah, but who pays any attention to it?" He took off his hat and scratched his head. "Jesus, as if there wasn't enough excitement for one day with the run on the bank and all."

"How did that turn out?" the Kid asked, then was interrupted by a knock on the door. "Go see who that is."

When Colfax unlocked the door, Nan Buckley stepped inside. "Is it true? Do you really have Rindo in jail?" She appeared to be on the verge of tears. "Oh, how humiliating! Are you trying to break his heart?"

"It'll heal quicker than his head," the Kid

said. "The crowd gone from the bank yet?"

"Yes," she said. Someone else knocked on the door and at the Kid's nod, she opened it.

A very agitated judge stepped quickly inside. Colfax turned the key again. Richmond puffed his cheeks and patted his chest gently. "Kid, this is highly irregular. I believe both parties can be released on their own recognizance."

"Maybe in the morning," the Kid said easily. "That way I'm sure of having one peaceful day."

"You mean you intend to keep them together in jail overnight?"

"Why not?" the Kid wanted to know. "Judge, here are two hellions who say they hate each other. Can't stand the sight of each other, to hear them tell it." He spread his hands innocently. "But due to an unfortunate disagreement with the law, they're forced to endure each other for twenty-some hours. Now it seems to me the main trouble is that they've never had a chance to sit down and either settle their differences or work up a genuine hate for each other. Well, I'm giving them that chance now."

"Most irregular," Richmond repeated.

"But a sound idea," the Kid insisted.

"Judge, could you get them together for a talk?"

"I doubt it," Richmond admitted. "You saw them awhile ago, dog-eyeing each other."

"That was in public," the Kid said. "A jail cell can be a mighty lonesome place at two in the morning when you can't sleep. You may hate the man in the cell next to you, but he's still someone to talk to."

"This from experience, Kid?" Colfax asked sarcastically.

The Kid looked quickly at him. "That election is still sticking in your craw, ain't it?"

The native resentments Ben Colfax held so close were evident in his eyes for a moment, then he drew his lids together, shutting them off from everyone. "I didn't like it," he said. "What the hell you expect?"

Judge Richmond shook his head and turned toward the door. "You have strange ways, sheriff. I haven't quite made up my mind what kind of man you are."

"You mean because I haven't taken sides?" He folded his arms across his chest. "Which side are you on, judge? Rindo's? Or the girl's? Or maybe you believe as I do, that neither of them matter; it's the town that's important."

Judge Richmond studied the Kid. Finally he said, "We all have sides, young man. A good side, and a bad one; we're an infernal blend. Occasionally it's difficult to say which side is predominant."

He went out quickly and Ben Colfax searched for an excuse to linger. "If you need me for anything —"

"I don't want a deputy," the Kid said. "How many times does a man have to tell you a thing before you understand it?"

This was calculated to sting, and it did, for angry color came into Colfax' face. He whirled to the door and slammed it after him. Nan Buckley said, "That was deliberate, Kid. You still don't like Ben, do you?"

"Less every day," the Kid said. He picked up the keys to the cell block and dropped them into his coat pocket. "Can I buy you a cup of coffee?"

"I'll make a better offer," she said. "Come home with me and I'll fix you something to eat."

He laughed and opened the door. "You'll never have to ask me twice," he said.

Traffic on the street appeared normal, and the groups gathered on the boardwalks were still laughing and discussing Rindo's arrest, giving the town a solid ballast; the earlier top-heavy condition seemed to have vanished.

At the *Rindo County Free Press* office, the printer and his devil were working on the paper, patiently setting the type in long sticks. Nan and the Kid passed into the rear; he took a place at the table while she stoked the fire. A gentle thought came to her and her lips pulled into a smile. "The town's come alive since you came here."

"Most of it unpleasant," he said, thinking of Pete and the desperation with which he had gone for his gun. "Do you believe all stories have happy endings, Nan?"

"Yes," she said. "Even the ones that seem sad to us. Happiness is relative. We usually gauge it from our own point of view, though." She placed a frying pan on the stove, added a dab of bacon grease, then cracked four eggs. "What are you thinking about, Kid?"

"The old man," he said. "He told me he wanted to give away what he owned before he died. I believe him."

"That sounds like something he'd do," Nan said.

"I've been doing a lot of figuring," the Kid admitted. "And I get some damned odd answers." He enumerated them on his fingers. "Now you take the original trouble between Bess's old man and Rindo. That was just talk until he was shot. But we know that Rindo didn't do it; I believe him when he claims he hired Pete as a threat, not to shoot anyone. Then the shooting of the teamster, that wasn't his doing either. Nan, I think both of them are victims of someone else who's got a lot to gain by seeing them get into a shooting fight."

She slid his eggs onto a plate, then sat down across from him. "But who'd do that?"

He shrugged and began to eat. "Did you ever think about money? I mean, what is money?" He fumbled through his pocket and brought out a paper bill. "Look at it. Just a piece of paper with ink on it. What makes it valuable?"

"It's backed by gold," she said.

"Oh, sure. If you take it to a bank, they'll give you gold for it. But suppose you're out on the desert and pay a man with this. The only reason he'll take it is because he has faith in what's behind it. At one time we all agreed to accept this as a thing of value. Hell, it could have been pieces of cut rock or beads, like the Indians used. The way I see it, Cadmus Rindo is that silent guarantee behind everything here. As long as he remains as is, Rindo's Springs will survive."

"But he's so old, Kid. He's bound to die before very long."

"Dying won't matter. That won't destroy what he was." He shook his head. "The danger is in his being undermined, making people doubt his backing. There's a difference between dying and being destroyed, Nan. And someone is out to do just that to the old man."

She remained silent while he ate the remainder of his eggs. Then she got up and poured him a cup of coffee. While he added sugar and milk, she observed him carefully. Finally she asked, "What happened to the Wind River Kid?" His eyes came up, surprised and a little puzzled. "You're not the same man, you know. The Wind River Kid was wise and tough and looking for trouble. The sheriff is quiet and thoughtful and never hunts trouble." She clasped her hands together and smiled. "You like Rindo's Springs, and I think the town likes you."

He liked the way this sounded, especially because she had said it, but then he remembered Cal Runyon and his pleasure vanished. She was quick to catch his changing moods and noticed this, but she failed to understand it. The Kid finished his coffee and got up. His manner was somewhat hurried as he gathered his hat and coat and turned toward the front of the building. She walked with him and at the door said, "I wish you liked me."

"Like you?" He ignored the printer and the scurrying devil. "Nan, it would be better if I could hate you." She stood near him, too near to ignore. Quickly he pulled her the rest of the way and folded his arms around her. She offered no resistance and didn't try to turn her face away from his kiss. The warmth and desirability of this woman ate at him, breaking down the walls of his resolve until he believed that her lips contained a promise for him alone.

When he released her, she looked steadily at him. The Kid said, "I don't think I ought to come here again." Before she could answer, he turned and started down the street. She came to the boardwalk's edge, her hand lifted as if to call him back, but then she thought better of it and went back inside.

Walking toward the restaurant, the Kid cursed himself for a fool. Any man was when he made love to a woman who belonged to another man. At the restaurant he ordered two meals and took them to the jail. Unlocking the barred doors, he placed a tray in each cell.

Bess Jamison said, "I suppose I should

thank you for this."

"Is there anyone you aren't sore at?" the Kid asked. "Just what did I ever do to you to deserve your smart talk? Tell me that."

"I don't have to like you," Bess said.

"And I don't have to take your smart mouth," the Kid told her. "Is it because I took the election away from Ben that you're peeved?"

"That's part of it," she admitted.

"Then why blame me? Did I have anything to do with it?"

"I guess you didn't," she said, after a pause.

"Then keep your tongue off me," he said, making his voice as tough as he could. That tone commanded respect from her and she kept watching him closely. "Get something straight: you don't have a solitary kick coming. When your teamster was killed, I caught the man who did it. You got justice all down the line, so stop your belly-achin'." He turned then and looked into the adjoining cell at Cadmus Rindo. "I suppose I've got to listen to you complain."

"The meal's good," Rindo said mildly. "No complaint."

"When are we going to get out of here?" Bess asked, her tone meek so he wouldn't misunderstand.

"You don't get out until the judge says so."

"When will that be?" Rindo asked.

"I'll try to find out sometime today," the Kid said, locking the doors again.

"When I get out, I'm going to take that badge away from you," Rindo promised. "You were just a drunk in jail when I pinned it on you. Just a gunfighter looking for a place to roost."

The Wind River Kid chuckled and went out, closing the separating door. After his step receded, Rindo said, "Damned smart guy."

"You elected him," Bess said dryly. "Stew in your own juice."

"Well, he's better'n Ben Colfax," Rindo snapped. "A dog's better'n him."

"How would you know? Any man that'd kill another —"

The old man flogged his thighs with his palms. "Jesus, are you still harpin' on that?" He made a disgusted noise with his lips. "The Kid didn't teach you a damned thing, did he? You still blame anyone in sight. Damned hollow-headed female, you can't recognize the truth when it's told to you!"

His voice had a genuine ring of truth which she could not completely ignore, and because the Kid had only a moment before shattered her anger, she had little left to color her thinking. "Who else had a reason to kill Pa?" she asked.

Rindo flung his hands in an aimless circle. "Damned if I know. I ain't even goin' to argue about it. Think what you please. Can't waste time tryin' to talk sense to someone who ain't got any."

Without realizing it, he was using a most successful attack, for Bess was not the kind of a woman who liked to be ignored or brushed aside. Her determination to talk now became almost an obsession. "Mr. Rindo, if I promise not to get angry, will you talk to me about — that night?"

For a moment it looked like he was going to refuse; then he blew out his breath and nodded. "No harm in it," he said. "But what's there to talk about?"

"About Pa," she said. "I don't think you understood him at all."

He stared at her, then laughed. "Didn't I? Hell, I had his number when I saw him come down the road in that old wagon. Everything he owned was patched, even the dress you had on, some hand-me-down you hoped no one would notice. Know him?" Rindo shook his head, amazed at her lack of perception. "Girl, there's a mark a man wears when he's a failure and too proud to admit it. I knew your father. Understood him, that's why I gave him timber of his own to cut; his kind never could work for anyone else, and didn't have the sand to stand up for himself."

He looked at her, challenging her to dispute this harsh judgment. "Girl, I didn't have to kill your father. If I'd wanted to get rid of him, all I would have had to do would be to blow hard and he'd have fallen down." He put his hands on his knees and bent forward, his voice softly spelling this out for her. "The thing that always bothered your pa was that he figured I'd not given him enough. It wasn't enough to work land and share the profit. He had to own it outright. That's been your bellyache all along. Callin' me an old hog, a tightwad." He laughed. "Think, girl. Be honest for once in your life. You knew your pa. Had he owned the land, he wouldn't have lasted a year. He'd have gotten the itch to move, to look at greener grass, and you'd have lost everything again."

She studied him with tear-bright eyes, for this was not a nice picture of any man. "How you must have loathed him!" she said.

"Still can't see your own nose, can you? No, I understood the man. And I had enough understanding to take his mouth and all the bricks he flung at me. Didn't feel sorry for him; he did that, enough for everyone. Girl, I was the only real friend your father had."

"Ben's been a friend," she said. "A real friend. I think that's why you dislike him so."

"Like tryin' to punch through a stone wall, talkin' to you," he said. "I know Ben's talk. He's convinced you that I'm afraid you'll get too big, take me over. Do you believe that?"

"What can I believe?" Bess asked. "Who can I believe?"

He stared at her, then got up and rattled the cell door until the Wind River Kid came back. "Got pen and paper?" Rindo asked.

"There's some in the desk," the Kid answered. "Going to make out your will?"

"Already done that," Rindo said. "Fetch me the writin' stuff."

The Kid returned to his office. A moment later he passed pen, ink, and paper into the cell. Cadmus Rindo carefully composed a neat page, then passed it back through the bars. "Read it," he said, "then sign it as a witness and give it to her."

As the Kid looked over the document, his interest sharpened. "This is a clear title to the property Bess is working. You sure you want me to sign it?"

"Sign it and give it to her," Rindo said.

After affixing his signature, the Kid passed it through the bars to Bess Jamison. She seemed stunned. "Why?" she asked softly. "After all this trouble, why?"

Rindo turned and looked at her. "Can't talk to you, so I'm teaching you the hard way. You've got what you said you wanted, but you won't hang onto it. There's too much of your father in you. I gave it to you so you could lose it, as he would have lost it. And when it's gone, pack your wagon and clear out of the country. I've done my last favor for the Jamisons."

Bess sat down and stared at the deed. She looked at the Kid, but he only said, "You're on your own now." Then he turned and went back to his office.

Seated behind his desk, he pondered Rindo's sudden and daring decision. The old man was no fool; there was grim purpose behind this move, and the Kid tried to fathom it. Of all those Rindo had helped, the Jamisons had come closer to building a power than anyone else. They cut a lot of timber in the Jamison camp, and there was another twenty years of logging in that section. Properly handled, that camp could take over in the event Rindo went under, and this thought touched off a new train in his mind.

Rindo knew that there was a quiet middle man working to ruin him through Bess Jamison, and the Kid had the notion that the free gift of the deed was a move to smoke that man into the open where he could be seen. A dangerous chance to take, the Kid decided. Too much of a chance for him to ever take, but then, there was the primary difference; Rindo being the kind of a man he was had carved an empire for himself while lesser men struggled just to live.

On impulse, the Kid left the office and went to the hotel. He found Wade Boomhauer reading. The young marshal put his magazine down and motioned toward a chair.

"How's your arm?" the Kid asked.

"Hurts like blue blazes," Boomhauer admitted. "Kid, I think you're sorry you shot me."

"Yes, I am." His fingers plucked at the brim of his hat. "You hear about me putting the old man in jail?"

Boomhauer chuckled. "The clerk wears out the steps bringing me the news." His laughter faded. "Think that was smart?"

"Yes," the Kid said. "I thought it was the right thing to do."

"As long as you believe that, you can't be far wrong." He paused to listen to the customary sounds drifting in the partially opened window. "The town's got a nice sound to it," he said. "Are you going to be able to hold it together?"

"Maybe."

"Kind of a new twist for you, isn't it? As I hear it, you've wrecked a few towns."

"This beats wrecking," the Kid said. He got up restlessly and put on his hat. "I may drop in and see you later."

"Then I'll look forward to it," Boomhauer said. When the Kid was half through the door, he added, "Taking you back is going to be one of the worst jobs I ever had."

The Kid's eyes were serious. "I'm not going to give you any more trouble, Wade."

"I figured that, which is what makes the job so bad."

The Kid closed the door and went down the stairs and through the lobby.

From his position on the boardwalk, he saw Cal Runyon leave the company yard, ride partway down the street, then turn onto the side street where Nan Buckley's newspaper office was. This brought back an old bitterness and he scuffed across the street toward the jail.

Faced with an extremely empty afternoon,

the Kid lay down on his cot and tried to sleep, but found it difficult. His mind kept swinging around to Nan Buckley, and visions of her in Cal Runyon's arms kept pushing to the fore, tormenting him almost beyond endurance. He was a fool, he told himself, to even consider for a moment that any woman could love a wanted man. Back in Arizona that crooked sheriff would have a judge waiting to give him four years. When he had served his time, he could drift again, without roots, without direction.

Sleep came unexpectedly and when he awoke he found the room growing dark. As he lighted the lamps, the door rattled beneath a man's heavy hammering and he opened it.

Five of Bess Jamison's men stood there, rifles and shotguns tucked in the crooks of their elbows. "She's been in long enough," one of the men said. "Let her out!"

"Come back in the morning," the Kid suggested. "I'll let her out then."

"We figure a few hours won't make a big difference," the leader said. He was a burly man, heavy in the face, with arms and shoulders thickened by a lifetime of felling timber.

"You fellas figure on breaking her out?" the Kid asked mildly.

"If you make us."

"Well," the Kid said, in a resigned voice, "I'm not going to buck armed men." He turned casually toward the door and the men began to surge forward, confident that this was going to be easy. Only the Kid turned the last step into a plunging leap that carried him inside. He slapped the oak door and slid the bar before they could react. Instantly they set up a clamor and he went to the gun rack, broke open a double-barrel shotgun and fed two brass, double-O buckshot loads into the chambers.

Then he went back to the door and suddenly flung it open.

The first man crowded forward, but stopped when the twin bores pressed hard against his chest. "Makes a big hole," the Kid said. "Want to see?"

"Ease back there," the man said to his friends. "Hal, will you stop that goddam shoving?" He looked apprehensively at the Kid.

A pushy man in back said, "Hell, Otis, break into him!"

"That's easy for you to say, but I got the barrels against my chest." This man remained motionless for a heartbeat longer, then edged back. At the boardwalk's edge, they lingered to save face, then shuffled off down the street.

Finally the Kid closed the door and put the shotgun away. Sitting down, he pillowed his forehead against his palms and let out a long, relieved breath. From the cell block, Bess Jamison called to him and he got up to see what she wanted.

"I thought I heard Otis' voice out there," she said.

"He wanted to break you out," the Kid said.

"Oh dear, now you don't think I put him up to that, do you?"

"No, but someone has done a lot of convincing somewhere along the line."

"I know that now," she said. Her look was contrite. "I've caused you a lot of trouble, haven't I?"

"Goes with the job," he said.

"Can I — do you suppose I could talk to Ben Colfax?"

"I haven't seen Ben all afternoon," the Kid admitted. "But if I find him, I'll say that you want to talk to him."

12

Seated again at his desk, the Kid turned his thoughts to Ben Colfax, the longtime friend and advisor to Bess Jamison and to her father before his death. Ben had a winning manner all right, but you couldn't condemn a man because he talked well. Then there was the matter of the poker games; Ben must have put in his share to stop the run on the bank.

The Kid rubbed the back of his neck, uncertain about his own speculations. While he thought about it, a bell began to toll insistently down the street, and he went to the front door to look out. Even as he stared down the street he heard Rindo's shout. But he had no time for Rindo now.

At the far end of town, the company buildings were making a high glow against the night sky, and a crowd began to race along the street at the firebell's call. The Kid broke into a run, pushing people aside who got in his way. Panting up to the main gate, he found it open and the guard absent. The main building was a sheet of flame and crumbling timbers, and company men were dashing about, trying to discover some avenue of attack. Sparks flew as the rising heat caused a wind, and other buildings caught. The crew at the stable drove the mules out of the compound as the haystack suddenly flared up.

The Kid searched for Cal Runyon and found him with Ben Colfax. Both men were studying the destruction as the Kid joined them. "What started this?" he asked.

"Wish I knew," Runyon said. "Ben was waiting for me in my office and I had scarcely closed the door when the bell rang." He turned to a man racing past. "You there! Get the men out of the yard! She's a goner!"

Talking was nearly impossible with the sound of the flames mounting to a roar. Runyon edged away, moving toward the main gate. The Kid and Colfax followed and when they could talk again, Runyon said, "I've got to see Cadmus Rindo!"

"All right," the Kid said and headed for the jail, "Will it be a total loss, Cal?"

"We may save something. All the livestock got clear. The buildings are gone, though."

"Going to be hard on Rindo's pocketbook," Ben Colfax opined.

"We'll make out," Runyon said, clearly indicating by his tone that he didn't want to talk about it.

"Sure knocks the props out from under the town," Colfax said. "The old man won't have anything to pay all the money the people have invested in him."

"I'll bet that makes you cry," the Kid snapped. "Why don't you go home, Ben? We don't want you around."

They were at the jail and went inside. Before the Kid could close the door, Colfax eased in. He had half a notion to throw him out, but he lacked the time. The Kid handed Runyon the keys to the cell block and the young superintendent went on ahead. The Kid could hear him talking.

"The buildings are all gone, Mr. Rindo."

"That bad, huh?" Springs squeaked as the old man eased off the cot. Then the cell door opened and Rindo came into the outer office.

Ben Colfax shifted his feet and said, "Mind if I talk to Bess?"

"No," the Kid said, then remembered. "She wanted to see you."

Colfax shuffled into the back and Cadmus Rindo sat down on the corner of the desk. "How did it get started?" Rindo asked.

"No one seems to know," Runyon admitted. "But of course there hasn't been time to talk to anyone and get a straight answer. Mr. Rindo, does this close us down? I mean, can we stand it, financially?"

"All empires are built on a shoestring," Rindo said flatly. "No, we can't float through this, not without the people's help. And they'll look after themselves first. Can't blame 'em. They're human."

From the rear came Bess' clear voice. "— but I tell you he gave it to me. No strings attached, Ben."

Then Ben Colfax came out of the cell block section and leaned against the wall. His eyes were tight-pinched and he looked carefully at Cadmus Rindo. "Nice thing you done, givin' Bess a clear title."

Rindo looked at him briefly, intolerantly. "What the hell is it to you anyway?"

"Considerable," Ben Colfax admitted. "You see, I got an investment there. Matter of fact, it's more'n an investment. You could say that I practically own it now, with this legal paper in my hand."

"What the hell's he saying?" Cal Runyon asked. He looked from the Kid to Rindo and then back to the Kid.

"Ben's been lending money," the Kid said.

"Just my generous nature," Ben said. "People like Bess and her pa have no business sense. Since I'm their friend, I handled it for 'em." He eased away from the wall. "Anyway, I'm still in business, and you're fresh out, Rindo." He smiled. "You shouldn't have run the Kid against me. I didn't like that. But then it gives me more pleasure to knock you down, old man."

"Get out of here," Rindo said. "I hate a sly man, and you've always been a sneak."

"Ah, that's hard talk," Colfax said. "But I'll go because I'm a man who don't want trouble." He stepped to the door and opened it. "Still, if you need money, come and see me. I'll buy up some of that paper these good folks are holding and when I get enough of it, I'll take over what's left of your mill."

"Where the hell did you ever get any money?" Runyon asked.

"Well," Colfax said, "I've been a peace officer a long time now. Must have arrested six or eight thousand drunks in my day. Always did like to pinch a drunk. Rarely ever give me any trouble, and most of 'em still have a little salted away on 'em someplace. Now and then I'd be disappointed and find only a quarter or a dollar. But over the years, even that counts up."

Cal Runyon was near enough to spit, and he did. Colfax' face turned concrete hard and he slowly raised his hand to wipe his cheek. "Shouldn't have done that," he said. "A bad thing to do to a man."

"Get out of here," the Kid said tightly.

"I'll see you too," Colfax promised and closed the door.

A deep silence filled the office for a time, then Cadmus Rindo smiled and said, "Look bright, boys. We rode high as hell while we stayed on her. We got no kick 'cause we got pitched off." He stood erect and stretched. "That cot's damned uncomfortable, Kid. Am I free to go or do I get locked up again?"

"You can go," the Kid said gently. The old man's courage in the face of disaster was a warming thing to see. Runyon still had the cell keys so the Kid said, "Go get Bess. Tell her she can go too."

When Runyon went down the hall, Rindo said, "Too bad you don't have some laid by. I'd like to see you buy up some of that stuff under Ben's nose."

"I wouldn't buy it," the Kid said. "Not because I don't think it would be a good investment, but because I still think I can save the town for you."

Rindo snorted. "Miracle worker, eh?" He turned as Bess came into the office. "You want to cheer, you go right ahead. Your friend's done a good job."

"I'm not cheering," she said softly. "I'm just ashamed for being so blind."

"A human failing," Rindo said and left.

Runyon said, "My place is with him, Kid." He glanced at Bess. "Are you staying in town?"

"If you want," she said.

"We have a lot to talk about," he said. "All right?"

"All right, Cal."

Bess dropped wearily into a chair, her expression troubled. "A lot of terrible possibilities are occurring to me," she said. "Are you wondering if Ben paid Pete to kill my father?"

He was surprised for it was almost as though she had read his thoughts. Going behind his desk, he opened the middle drawer and brought out the box of tagged bullets and spread them on the desk. Two he could ignore for they merely marked the fatality of itinerants. The other three merited his concern. He spaced them out in their correct order: Pritchard's first, then Jamison's, and finally the teamster's; he felt a pang of shame because he didn't even know the man's name.

Then he recalled the bullet Doc Carver

had given him at the inquest and sounded his pockets until he came up with it. He laid this too on the desk, with no more than half a glance, but that was enough for a man who had made guns and bullets his business.

For a full minute he stared at the bullet. Bess Jamison asked, "What's wrong? You look odd."

"This *is* odd," he said. "If Doc hasn't made a mistake with his tag, I shot Pete with his own gun. And that's impossible because I didn't find it until I came back to Rindo's Springs."

He pawed his mouth out of shape, flogging his mind to recall — then recollection came full bloom and he slapped the desk with the flat of his hand. "How damned stupid can a man get!" He turned and looked at Bess's expectant expression. "I didn't shoot Pete with his own gun. I shot him with the one Ben Colfax loaned me after I dropped mine in the mud in front of the newspaper office."

"I — I don't understand."

"And I'm just beginning to," the Kid said. "Bess, I'll try and put this together for you. First, Ben shot your father. Yes, he did, and I can prove it. And he shot the teamster, then swore it was Pete who did it. When he brought the body back to town, he loaned me his gun so I could go after Pete. Then when he heard I was comparing bullets, he had to do something to make the case complete against Pete. He must have gone to the stable, put his own odd-caliber Colt in Pete's saddlebag, the one chambered for .44 American, then led me by the nose so I'd find it." He shook his head. "Guns are my business, and I guess there isn't a caliber in the handguns that I haven't shot at one time or another, but I'll be switched if I noticed any difference in weight or recoil when I shot Pete. Ben probably weighed the butt just right to make it balance." He wiped his hand across his mouth. "Then too, the gun being a Colt threw me off; it felt right and natural to my hand. And when a man gets mixed up in a shooting scrape, he's too keyed up to notice a little thing like recoil. You know, it all fits in because Ben's got the nerve to take a long chance like that, slipping in the murder weapon right under my nose. I played poker with him once and I watched him fill inside straights. The man's cool and he won't break under fire." The Kid smiled. "When I started to compare bullets, Ben must have had a bad moment, for I was walking around with the murder gun on my hip. But he never lost his head." He stood up slowly. "Better get on over to the hotel, Bess. I've got a man to arrest."

"Do you think he'll — fight?"

"Yes," the Kid said. "Ben'll fight. He played a quiet game for mighty big stakes, and he still has a chance to win. That's the bad part of it."

"I — I don't know what to say. He seems like a stranger now, as though I never really knew him at all."

"Perhaps you didn't," he said. "Bess, how much do we really know of anyone? We think we do, putting all kinds of interpretations on what they say and do, but do we really know them?"

"I suppose not," she said and went to the door. "Should I tell anyone what I know about Ben?"

He considered this briefly. "Yes, spread it around. Let's see if we can make Ben run."

After she left he took his revolver and checked it thoroughly, for in a short time now, he would need it. He felt a desire to go outside and feel the pulse of the town, but he was afraid to. The fire at the mill would shatter the strength of these people and he found little pleasure in the prospect of seeing them go down.

This would be more than the end of a

town. This was the end of Jim Onart, a man with self-respect; after tonight, if he didn't make a fatal mistake with Ben, he would be the Wind River Kid, riding back to Arizona with a pair of handcuffs on his wrists and a most undecided future.

While he sat there with his dismal thoughts, the first rumble of thunder sounded in the northeast and a moment later a few raindrops splattered on the roof. Soon it set up a dull roar and made sagging patterns on the front windows.

A miserable night, he decided, then put on his hat and coat and went outside. He wondered if Ben Colfax was moving around, trying to make his quick deals, buying up Cadmus Rindo's notes. Very likely. The man wouldn't waste any time; he'd glean his reward here as avariciously as he swept poker winnings into his corner.

The street was empty, as far as traffic went, but most of the stores were still open and the Kid started his rounds, hunting. He chose the dry goods store first because it was the closest. The proprietor was a prune-dry man and about as angry as one man could be. He puffed and glared at the sheriff and snapped, "If you're after the old man's notes too, they ain't for sale!"

This attack, out of nowhere, rocked the

Kid. "What's the matter? Ben's money no good?"

"Damned right it's no good! Worthless! I spit on it!"

"Ben's been here then?"

"Twenty minutes ago. Was I a bigger man I'd have flung him into the street."

Bewildered, the Kid left the store and started up the street. He stopped at three places and was surprised at their vehemence. In the butcher shop, the rotund butcher said, "You think I'd kick a man who's down? That ain't a very good opinion of me, sheriff. Hell, I've been down too. You think I'd ever forget what Rindo done for me?"

A glimmer of hope began to warm the Kid. By the time he covered the other side of the street, he began to understand these people and their mass, concentrated outrage. How many plots had been hatched here to wrest control from Rindo he could only guess. How much time had they wasted, complaining, threatening; this was a mystery to him. And he had blamed them, thought them evil, when all the time they had been merely human. It had never occurred to him that these people would unite, but they had, arming themselves against this intruder, Ben Colfax.

And Cadmus Rindo was right after all. He had given his best to all men and because of this, they offered him the best in return. People, the Wind River Kid decided, were magnificent if only a man stopped long enough to notice instead of digging at the dirt that was under every man's fingernails.

He wondered if Rindo knew how these people felt. The man must know or else he would never have been able to live out his advanced years under so mellow a philosophy.

But this was no time to wax sentimental; the Kid pulled his mind back to Ben Colfax, for the news was out now and circulating like wildfire. From down the street, the Kid saw Judge Richmond and Dr. Carver moving head-down against the rain. They saw him at the last minute and veered toward the shelter of the overhang.

"You're the man we want to see," Richmond said. He pulled a folded paper from his inner pocket. "Here is a warrant for Ben Colfax' arrest. Do you need any help?"

"I can handle it," the Kid said. "That's what the county pays me for."

"We can get a citizen's committee," Doc Carver said. "God, I never saw them so riled before!"

"Their security has been threatened," Richmond said. "For twenty years I've been a public servant and never an election has passed but what I wasn't cussed and booed. But that's our privilege, sheriff."

"Getting Ben is my job," the Kid said.

"And it won't be easy," Carver said. "What can we do to help?"

"I've been thinking about it," the Kid admitted, "and I've come to the conclusion that there's too many people on the streets. If you gents could move around and ask the merchants to close and lock their doors, but leave the lights on, I could have this town to myself. Simply by keeping everyone indoors, I can catch Ben a lot easier."

"And if there's any shooting, no one will get hurt," Richmond said. He was a practical man who considered the chances carefully. "Ben's pretty good. He doesn't make much of a point of it, but he is."

The Kid moved his hand impatiently. "See how quick you can clear the street."

They hurried on and the Kid turned toward the hotel. Without understanding why, he felt the need to talk to Boomhauer. He knocked and went in. The clerk was there with the supper tray and the latest news. At the marshal's nod, the clerk left, then Boomhauer said, "A good job, sheriff.

You ought to be proud of it."

"Not finished yet," the Kid said. "I got the merchandise laid out but there's still the wrapping."

"Ummm," Boomhauer said, smiling. "I've been tangled in those strings myself. Made any plans?"

"I've got the judge and the doctor clearing the street. That way, with just Ben and me moving about, I'll know who to shoot at."

"A sensible move," Boomhauer said. "Can I offer a little advice, Kid?"

"That's what I came here for."

Boomhauer propped himself up on his elbow, then pushed until he sat up. Then he opened the front of his long underwear and exposed an old bullet wound on his chest. "Thought I'd show you this first to make an impression," he said. "Kid, this is going to be different. No walk-up here, and it's the first man that sees the other, not who is fastest."

"Figured that," the Kid said. "But I shoot straight enough."

"And if you're thinking that the other man might not, then you're not as smart as I thought you were. Kid, you're a lawman tonight, not a gunfighter defending his reputation. Forget the damned code or whatever you go by and think. You got a rifle?"

"No," the Kid said.

"Mine's in the closet. There's a box of shells in the canvas satchel. That rifle's a .50–110 Winchester Express and she'll shoot through six inches of oak. Eight rounds, instead of five, and you don't have to get into pistol range." He reached out and took the Kid by the sleeve. "If he gets behind a door, your sixgun is worthless. Go get the rifle."

The Kid obeyed and was impressed by the gun's murderously efficient lines. He checked the magazine and found it to be full. He put the box of shells in his coat pocket, but Wade Boomhauer had a criticism. "Take the shells out of the box and carry them loose. If you need 'em, you won't have time to fool with the box."

After doing this, the Kid said, "This doesn't give Ben much of a chance, does it?"

"This evens your chances," Boomhauer said flatly. "Kid, you've got to tree this lion on the ground of his choosing. Looking for him gives him a tremendous advantage." When the Kid tucked the Winchester under his arm, Boomhauer asked, "Can you shoot that?"

"Pretty good," the Kid said and moved to the door. "Thanks. You knew what I needed."

"Be careful and think," Boomhauer said sternly. "It cost me this dimple on the chest to find out what I just told you."

A smile was the Kid's answer and he tromped down the stairs. The clerk had locked the front door and he let the sheriff out, then turned the key behind him. A glance at the street was sufficient to show that Richmond and Carver had done a complete job; the Wind River Kid was alone with his adopted town.

What was the best way, he wondered. Taking each side in turn, or the alley first? The alleys, he decided, for he had no way of knowing where Ben was hiding. And he was fairly certain he would be hiding now. Or perhaps not; the Kid was recalling the poker game — much of the man had been revealed in those few hours.

Ben, he felt sure, would not run; he was not the kind who backed down. No, he'd want to square this, just as surely as he tried to win back a lost hand at cards.

But where would a man in his position wait? Not the stable; too crowded. The street too was unlikely. Then the Kid hit on it and started for the burned-out company yard. The rain had done more in fifteen minutes toward putting out the fire than all of the company buckets put together. As the Kid approached the still open main gate, he observed the clouds of steam rising from the black rubble. There was an almost constant hissing as the rain sought out still-live embers.

The night was ink dark here, and he moved into the main yard, angling toward the spot where the main company building had once stood. Farther out, the barracks remained intact; bright squares of light indicated that they were occupied. For over a half-hour he moved around carefully but saw no one. The stable area was devastated, and he searched there thinking that perhaps Ben would take one of the horses. Leaving the stable, he cruised about what was left of the saw and planing mill. The fire had destroyed everything but the heat-bent machinery; this loomed black and useless now.

The Kid put the barracks out of his mind; Ben Colfax would want a dark spot. In an hour, he had covered the whole grounds and found nothing, which puzzled him to the point of disappointment for he had been sure that Colfax would take refuge —

He stopped and stood absolutely motionless. In the rush of hunting his man he had failed to take into consideration the things he had learned about Ben Colfax: the man's cold nerve, his desperate courage. And on the heels of this came the jarring thought that Ben would never run and hide. He would play with a man, double back on him, turn the hunter into the hunted.

The Kid stood in the muddy yard, looking about, trying to determine a logical place to make his stand; he was determined not to let Ben Colfax pick it, yet the man would if he could. Doubling back, the Kid ran past the ruined slab furnace and on to the fire-damaged machinery, there stopping. He paused to still his breathing and wipe a hand over his face. The night was thick with black shadows, and the Kid felt like a country yokel trying to pick the shell that hid the all-important pea. Colfax was in possibly a dozen spots; the Kid could only move about and take a chance on Ben missing his first shot.

As he approached the burned-out harness shop, the Kid stopped, for he saw an odd-shaped shadow. He had the rifle in his right hand and started to lift it, then stopped when Ben Colfax said, "Nope, nope! Wouldn't do that if I was you."

He eased into the clear then and the Kid

saw that Ben Colfax did not have a gun in his hand. "This going to be even, Ben?"

"Well now, no draw is ever really even," Ben said. "The trouble with you young fellas is that you don't take an older man's advice. I told you a couple of times that I was pretty good, but since I didn't pull on everyone, you thought I was lyin'."

"You're a pretty good liar, Ben."

"In some things I be," Colfax admitted, "but in others I ain't." He chuckled. "You want to look at yourself, you'll see that I've got you on the hip for sure. A rifle ain't your weapon, son, yet you're standing there holding it in your sixgun hand. Now you ain't free to draw your sixgun, and you're going to be clumsy with that rifle, so I'll let you just go ahead and make up your mind which one you're going to use. When you go for either, I'll get you." He lifted his right hand a little. "You go ahead any time you're ready, Kid."

Some decisions, the Kid decided, were already made for you, and he did not hesitate. Flipping the rifle from his right hand to the left, he drew and knew that he was beat before the pistol started to slip from the leather. Ben Colfax hadn't been lying about his speed and the Wind River Kid launched himself into the mud as Ben shot. The bullet struck either his gun or his hand; with the sudden numbness he could not be sure which had been hit.

He was in the mud and rolling and Ben shot twice more before the Kid could heft his rifle into play. Then he was too late — Colfax was running, dodging amid the wreckage, and then he was gone.

Sitting up, the Kid looked at his right hand and saw that he was not bleeding. He found his sixgun but it was hopelessly jammed. Thrusting it back into the holster, he stood there and wondered where a man went from here. Was he going to do this all over again, smoke Ben out again, or let the man go, giving it up for a bad deal. The answer was simple; he'd hunt Ben until he found him.

Hunt where? Where, he asked himself, would a man go and be sure he was safe? The answer was so clear that it became a little frightening. Breaking into a trot, he slogged across the muddy yard and headed for Cadmus Rindo's house. The rain had soaked completely through his clothes now but he was hardly aware of the discomfort.

Out of deference, the citizens of Rindo's Springs would leave the old man alone in this hour of tragedy, and a safer place couldn't be found if Ben wanted to hole up.

And Ben was smart enough to figure this out.

Approaching Rindo's house, the Kid circled once and saw that it was brightly lighted, which in itself was unusual. There was no way, the Kid decided, in which to sneak into the house; the windows shed light on the grounds all around the house.

So he used the bold approach, knocking on the front door. A moment later he heard Rindo's shuffling step, then the door opened. The old man said, "I'm tired, Kid. Come back tomorrow."

The absence of the servant warned the Kid that he had pulled in a good hand. Now all he had to do was play it into a winner. Rudely he brushed past the old man and stepped into the hall. Common sense told him that Ben was close at hand; he'd never let the old man out of his sight. Rindo licked his lips nervously and because he offered no nod, the Kid was positive that his guess had been a good one.

The library was out; an arch opened up there. On the other side was a heavy oak door that led to another part of the house. At the end of the hall another heavy door was slightly ajar; the Kid needed no other clue.

Suddenly flailing out with his arm, he

caught Cadmus Rindo in the chest, flinging him against the wall. Instantly the snout of a pistol came out of the door crack and the Kid worked the lever of the Winchester.

Ben Colfax got off the first shot, a good one that snapped past the Kid's cheek and buried in the woodwork. Then the Kid touched off the .50–110 Winchester Express and the room bulged with the concussion. He didn't stop to see how good his shot was, just worked the lever hurriedly and puckered the door five times, showering that end of the hall with splinters.

There was another shot fired, when Colfax caved at the knees and triggered one off into the rug. The door flew wide and Colfax sprawled, bleeding from four ragged holes.

Slowly, Cadmus Rindo picked himself up from the floor and rubbed the spot where the Kid had hit him. Then he slapped his ears to still the ringing. "Damn," he said, "when you come in I liked to had a stroke! You'd have never shot through that door with a six pistol."

The Kid walked over and looked down at Ben Colfax, shot through and through. Then he turned to the old man. "He couldn't buy one dollar's worth of paper," he said. "The town turned on him like a pack of wolves."

The old man tipped his head forward slowly and stood that way, his chin nearly touching his chest. In a moment he hauled a huge blue handkerchief from his hip pocket and blew noisily. "Damned wet weather," he said. "Can't take it like I used to."

"I'll send someone over to get Ben out of here," the Kid said. Rindo nodded once and the Kid let himself out. With the cold rain against his face, he realized that he was sweating. He cradled the weighty Winchester in his arms and then walked back to the hotel.

A great sadness pressed on him, and yet a new sense of peace helped lift him. This was the end of the road. As far as a man could go, and it really didn't matter now what that Arizona judge handed him, for he had taken his place among men, and proved to himself that he wasn't as bad as some people thought.

He found Richmond and Carver in the hotel lobby. In a quiet voice, he said, "Send a couple of the boys to Rindo's house to pick up Ben."

"He was there?" Carver blurted out.

The Kid nodded. "Probably figured to shoot the old man after he got me."

"We owe you —" Richmond began, but

the Kid was moving away toward the stairs. At the judge's nod, Carver went out.

Not bothering to knock, the Kid let himself into Boomhauer's room. He found the marshal sitting up by the window, pants and boots on.

"That's a good rifle," the Kid said. He set it carefully in the closet, then took the shells from his pocket and replaced them in the box. "In a couple of days you'll feel good enough to travel, huh?"

"Maybe," Boomhauer said. "How do you feel, Kid?"

"Feel?" the Kid shrugged. "Better. Better than when I came here."

"Well, you gave these people a little of yourself," Boomhauer said. "Not many men can do that." He turned around and looked at the badly tarnished badge sagging from the Kid's coat. "Why the hell don't you polish that thing? Where's your pride?"

"Just a temporary job," the Kid said. "Besides, it'll tarnish again."

This seemed to make Wade Boomhauer a little angry; he gave the Kid a blunt stare. "Don't you learn anything? Jesus, man, we all tarnish. One of the biggest jobs in life is to keep polishing." He closed his mouth when a knock shook the door. "It's open."

Nan Buckley stepped inside, her face

grave. "They told me I'd find you here, Kid." Her glance touched Boomhauer, wished him long gone, then swung back to the Kid. "Were you going to leave without saying anything?"

"I saw Cal Runyon heading toward your place today," he said. He shook his head. "We'd better not say anything more about it, Nan."

"Don't you want to hear what I have to say?"

Now she was testing his fairness. He said, "Sure, Nan."

"I told him that we'd made a mistake," Nan said. "I told him that I loved you, Kid. I said that when you went to Arizona that I was going too, and when you got out of prison, I'd be there waiting to marry you."

The Kid looked at her with the expression of a man who had been stoned between the eyes. Wade Boomhauer cleared his throat and they both looked at him as though they just recalled that he was there.

"He accepts," Boomhauer said, smiling faintly. "Miss, whenever a man looks that stupid, he's accepted." He made a motion toward the night stand. "I had the clerk bring me a telegraph blank. Would you hand it to me, please? And the pencil there too."

With an effort the Wind River Kid performed this simple service, then watched as Boomhauer wrote his message. He handed it to Nan Buckley and said, "You run a newspaper. Are there any misspelled words there? Got to keep official correspondence neat."

She read it, a tense expression on her face. When she finished she said, "Can he read it too?"

"Sure," Boomhauer said, patting his pockets for a cigar. The message read:

United States Marshal
Tucson, Arizona Territory
Unable to locate Wind River Kid these parts.
Believe original information to be false.
   (signed) **Boomhauer, U.S. marshal**

The Kid handed the message back. "Why, Wade? What about all that stuff, being a lawman and doing your duty?"

"You damn fool," Boomhauer said without anger. "I just did it. Now get the devil out of here and let me enjoy my cigar and my view of the town."

"We'll have a quiet funeral for the Wind River Kid," Nan said softly.

"Make it real quiet," Boomhauer said. "I

want to sleep late in the morning."

He laughed when they went out, closing the door.

ABOUT THE AUTHOR

Will Cook is the author of numerous outstanding Western novels as well as historical frontier fiction. He was born in Richmond, Indiana, but was raised by an aunt and uncle in Cambridge, Illinois. He joined the U.S. cavalry at the age of sixteen but was disillusioned because horses were being eliminated through mechanization. He transferred to the U.S. Army Air Force in which he served in the South Pacific during the Second World War. Cook turned to writing in 1951 and contributed a number of outstanding short stories to *Dime Western* and other pulp magazines as well as fiction for major smooth-paper magazines such as *The Saturday Evening Post.* It was in the *Post* that his best-known novel *Comanche Captives* was serialized. It was later filmed as *Two Rode Together* (Columbia, 1961) directed by John Ford and starring James Stewart and Richard Widmark. Sometimes in his short stories Cook would introduce characters that would later be featured in novels, such as Charlie Boomhauer who first appeared in *Lawmen Die Sudden* in *Big-Book Western* in 1953 and is later to be found in *Badman's Holiday* (1958) and *The Wind River Kid* (1958). Along with his steady productivity, Cook maintained an enviable quality. His novels range widely in time and place, from the Illinois frontier of 1811 to southwest Texas in 1905, but each is peopled with credible and interesting characters whose interactions form the backbone of the narrative. Most of his novels deal with more or less traditional Western themes — range wars, reformed outlaws, cattle rustling, Indian fighting — but there are also romantic novels such as *Sabrina Kane* (1956) and exercises in historical realism such as *Elizabeth, by Name* (1958). Indeed, his fiction is known for its strong heroines. Another common feature is Cook's compassion for his characters who must be able to survive in a wild and violent land. His protagonists made mistakes, hurt people they care for, and sometimes succumb to ignoble impulses, but this all provides an added dimension to the artistry of his work.

We hope you have enjoyed this Large Print book. Other Thorndike, Wheeler, and Chivers Press Large Print books are available at your library or directly from the publishers.

For information about current and upcoming titles, please call or write, without obligation, to:

Publisher
Thorndike Press
295 Kennedy Memorial Drive
Waterville, ME 04901
Tel. (800) 223-1244

or visit our Web site at:

www.gale.com/thorndike
www.gale.com/wheeler

OR

Chivers Large Print
published by BBC Audiobooks Ltd
St James House, The Square
Lower Bristol Road
Bath BA2 3SB
England
Tel. +44(0) 800 136919
email: bbcaudiobooks@bbc.co.uk
www.bbcaudiobooks.co.uk

All our Large Print titles are designed for easy reading, and all our books are made to last.